CIRCLE H RANGE

**Center Point
Large Print**

**This Large Print Book carries the
Seal of Approval of N.A.V.H.**

CIRCLE H RANGE

LAURAN PAINE

Center Point Publishing
Thorndike, Maine

This Center Point Large Print edition
is published in the year 2005 by arrangement with
Golden West Literary Agency.

Copyright © 2005 by Mona Paine.
Copyright © 1976 in the British Commonwealth.

All rights reserved.

The text of this Large Print edition is unabridged. In other
aspects, this book may vary from the original edition. Printed in
Thailand. Set in 16-point Times New Roman type.

ISBN 1-58547-529-7

Library of Congress Cataloging-in-Publication Data

Paine, Lauran.
    Circle H range / Lauran Paine.--Center Point large print ed.
        p. cm.
    Originally published in Great Britain under the pseudonym of John Durham.
    ISBN 1-58547-529-7 (lib. bdg. : alk. paper)
        1. Large type books. I. Title.

PS3566.A34C55 2005
813'.54--dc22

                                                        2004014991

Chapter One
ONE SICK COW

Charley's grizzled, seamed and weathered face showed plainly that he did not want to do what had to be done. But there was also a hint of resignation in his steely grey eyes as he stood with Young Jim, their horses fifty feet to the rear, watching the cow.

She was flat down, sweaty, feeble from prolonged labor, and although she rolled her eyes at them and would have waggled her wicked-horned head in warning, if she'd had the strength, she was too far gone in exhaustion, too weak and sick to even lift her head from the grass.

Charley began unbuttoning his shirt as he said, 'If we'd missed her for another day she'd be dead.' He made that statement flatly, not entirely because he wished they *had* missed riding up onto her, but not happy that they had, either.

He dropped the shirt, tossed down his hat, growled for Young Jim to fetch one of the lariats, then stepped behind the enormously distended carcass and sank to his knees as he rolled the arm of his long-underwear to the shoulder, tough-set his lips and went to work.

The cow did not appear to even feel it when he ran his hand and half his arm inside her. Once, though, she struggled to make one last effort at expelling the calf. It was far too weak an effort, even if the calf had been able to arrive normally, which it could not have, because one foreleg was cocked back.

Young Jim returned with the rope, and stared as Charley leaned, shoving with all his weight to reach deeper. He sighed. 'Got it; give me the slip-knot-end.' He reared back, straining hard, bringing not just the bent leg, but its mate, with his withdrawing fist. It was hard work, but worse, it was unpleasant and awkward work. Young Jim handed down the lariat, Charley got it firmly snugged up over both slimy front legs, then growled at the lanky youth. 'Let go some slack. Walk back ten feet behind me, dig in, and when I raise my hand, you set to and pull hard. When I drop my arm, quit pulling . . . Ready?'

Young Jim muttered and slid rope through his gloved hands. Sweat dappled his face, and not entirely because this was midsummer out in the middle of eight thousand acres of grassland with no shade and the yellow sun directly overhead.

Charley raised his hand, kneeling. When Young Jim set back the calf's nose showed, but Charley had to work the flesh back, hard, in order for the head to squeeze past. He swore, on the verge of reaching into a trouser pocket for his clasp-knife, when Young Jim's steady pressure pulled the head free. After that, the calf's body slid forth like a wet, black, snake.

The cow groaned and fell limp. Charley yanked loose the lariat, working swiftly. By all rights, the calf should have been dead. It wasn't, but the flicker of life was dim, which was why Charley worked fast freeing the nostrils, casting aside the rope and jumping to his feet. 'Grab a hind leg,' he barked at the lanky cowboy. 'Never mind the rope, drop it and grab a hind leg.

That's it, now stand up straight.'

They hung the calf between them, upside down. It was heavy, but worse, it was too slippery for a good grip and Young Jim had to use both hands.

Fluid ran from the little animal's nostrils and mouth. Charley watched with the shrewd interest of an experienced stockman. When they had held the calf head-down long enough he said, 'All right; now we'll carry it up front and leave it in the grass beside the cow's head.'

They accomplished this, the cow rolled bloodshot eyes again, and Charley smiled flintily at her. 'You damned old fool, you must've had ten of these things in your time—why get into trouble this time?' He went back after his shirt, dumped the hat upon the back of his head and looked back where the horses were standing. 'Let's ride to the creek,' he said, without wasting another glance at the cow and her weakly moving big, wet, red calf.

They had a mile to ride and neither of them said a word until they dismounted in among the leaving willows to get down and scrub clean in the cold water. Then Charley looked over at the gangling youth.

'Next time it's your turn.'

Young Jim did not raise his eyes from the creek as he washed both hands vigorously. He did not utter a word. Beneath the layers of sun-tan there was a hint of paleness.

Charley understood, but he was a hard, gruff man. At fifty-five he was over the hill for a rangerider, but no one ever said this to his face, and he certainly never said it to himself, so he kept signing on for each riding season.

7

He had done it all, at one time or another. He was a tophand and had been one for twelve years. Only once, had he ever been a rangeboss in all his years on the ranges. There had been a reason for this, but that was something else a man never reproached himself about. In cow-savvy, he was the equal of any cowman, rangeboss, or cowboy, but he always hired on as tophand and nothing more.

Charley also had a way with horses, and with men. He had never been married, knew practically nothing about children or pigs, and was content to have his life so ordered.

Young buckaroos just starting out were something different. In Charley Wagner's time he had probably started as many of them as he had green colts, and he handled both the same way, with firmness, understanding, and a no-nonsense attitude which called for hard work and absolute honesty.

If Charley had ever been a complicated man, by the time he would admit to fifty years, he had become settled, forthright, very limited in imagination, and predictable. Perhaps once he had had illusions; most cowboys imagine themselves as cow*men,* ranchowners, some time in their lives. A few of them achieve it, and most of them are still thinking it could happen the morning they arise and go out back to shave, and discover grey in their hair. They know then it is not going to happen.

Charley may have done this. On the creek-bank in willow shade with Young Jim, lolling back where it was cool, listening to the sound of hurrying water, and smoking, Charley almost admitted that he had once owned the cowboy's dream.

He had patiently explained about the pulled-calf, then he had said, 'It never was all ridin', son, not even back when you dassn't ride too near a forest or some warwhoop'd shoot you out of the saddle. It takes a long while to learn enough so's when you get up where you're aiming, you'll know when to do whatever's got to be done.' He exhaled blue smoke, which hung in the heavy, utterly still air, let his perpetually narrowed eyes drift back to the opposite side where more creek-willows grew, and smiled a little, while adding a final statement.

'And when you get there, hell, it's not the place you had in mind at all.'

He flipped the cigarette into the water, watched it twist and turn as it was borne away, then grunted up to his feet and put on his shirt. He only owned two, and the other one was dirty, back at the bunkhouse, otherwise he might not have removed it prior to pulling the calf.

Young Jim looked older than he was, from a distance, because he stood better than six feet tall, was big-boned and rode straight-up in the saddle. When they walked back to get astride he looked over at the shorter, thicker man, a question in his mind.

'Charley, what's worse than pulling a calf?'

The older man grunted up, settled square, and urged his horse towards home, with the sun dropping a little away over his left shoulder. 'You'll find out one of these days,' he replied. 'Sometimes a cow don't clean out; she don't slip that big wet sack the calf's folded into while

9

she's carrying it. It's supposed to slough off when the calf's born, or maybe a day or so later. When it don't— well—you rope the cow, snub her nose to a tree or a post, and you peel down like I done with the calf, and reach inside and peel all that stuff off them little round buttons deep inside her.' Charley glanced at the staring youth. 'Mostly, you'll notice cows that ain't cleaned out because they got that stuff trailing out of them. Sometimes it's because the flies are following them so thick.' Charley kept looking at Young Jim. 'That stuff rots inside 'em, and it gags a man having to get right up there and do the job.' His gaze did not relent. 'We'll find one, someday. I'll show you.'

Young Jim dumbly nodded and was silent until they got back out where the cow was weakly standing, legs wide, with her pulled-calf nuzzling her side. She shook her horns in warning and Charley smiled back at her. As they skirted out and around he called to her.

'It's all right now, old girl, but you'd better not do that next year.' He turned slowly from watching the cow and calf. 'I usually notch an ear so's I'll know which cows get hung up, then we include them into the bunch we trail out to rails-end each autumn.'

Young Jim glanced back. 'Why didn't you do it to her?'

Charley shrugged thick shoulders. 'Well, hell, she's had a lot of calves. She's entitled to one mistake.' He peered ahead and swiftly changed the subject. 'Someone turned out the remuda.'

A band of sleek, playful saddle animals were racing towards them from the direction of the ranch, but they shied wide, split into two groups and raced past the riders on each side as though they had never seen mounted men before.

Charley smiled. A lifetime on the ranges had taught him to think like a horse, when he saw horses, and otherwise to think like a cow. 'Someday, someone's going to figure out a way to bottle that wasted energy, then a man'll be able to walk into a store and buy himself some of it.'

Young Jim slowly grinned. He rarely laughed aloud and seldom smiled, but occasionally he would grin when something tickled him. 'How would they ever do that?' he challenged. 'Feelin' good isn't nothing you can *see* to catch, Charley.'

The older man's narrowed eyes turned speculative. 'Well now, Young Jim, you can't see the air, either, can you? Hell, son, a man can't *see* a whole rangeful of things which he uses. You know, when I was about your age, I wintered one time with a party of Hidatsas— them's the Sioux they call "big bellies" because they eat all their kinsmen out of house and home when they go visiting. There was an old man in that camp, and all winter long he told me stories. One story was about a big bloody-hand bronco buck—best warrior in the world, according to the old man, and he met this bird in a forest one day, and the bird told him how to braid his hair so bullets couldn't harm him. So the bronco fixed his hair just right, and hell, he went off on raid after raid, and sure enough, no one could hit him. Then one day a Crow threw a tomahawk at this bronco buck and split his breastbone neat as a whistle, so the bronco buck died—and you know what the old man told me? He said the bronco buck was foolish; he should have expected that Crow to throw his axe; he said anything can happen to a man when he can't see it coming, but in this life only fools get killed by things they can see.'

Young Jim rode the balance of the distance back to the ranch trying to puzzle his way through that. He was too polite to ask Charley for an explanation, and Charley never mentioned the bronco buck again.

Chapter Two
A MAN'S WORLD

It was a big country. Across the grasslands stood mountains with sides and slopes which gradually lifted for twenty miles before they achieved any kind of a top-out. A man could ride for a week, if he had to, or if he chose to, and see nothing but horses, cattle, wild game and an occasional horseman.

The town sat near some westerly slopes and was made entirely of wood; some older log structures still existed, but mostly, Kremmling had board-and-bat buildings.

Its streets were very wide, and bordered on each side by perfectly flat plankwalks which were not especially needed this time of year, summer, but were all that stood between a muddy morass and dry feet in wintertime.

In a place as isolated, and in a country as large and empty, people were names more than personalities; George Hinman, for example, who owned all the country beginning four miles beyond Kremmling north and west, to the top of the heat-hazed, blurry peaks, with four hired hands, fifty head of using horses and three thousand head of cattle, was known throughout the territory, and especially down in Kremmling, even though a month might pass without his ever appearing in town.

The same was true of other large landholders and cowmen. People mentioned their names often enough without actually seeing them very often. The reason was simple: Cow outfits were usually called by the name of their brand—the Hinman mark was Shield H, a big circle, left ribs, with a large H in the centre of it—but just as frequently they were known by their owner's name, as 'the Hinman place', or 'the Jones place', and when a man's name signified something as large and substantial as perhaps eight to fifteen thousand acres of land, the man whose name it bore assumed some out-sized proportions, as though he were twelve feet tall and correspondingly wide.

Actually, George Hinman was slightly less than average in height, and although he was bull-built, like his tophand Charley Wagner, and even to some degree resembled Charley, being grizzled and lined and hard-eyed, in any large city George Hinman would have been overlooked. He was no more outstanding in appearance than Charley was.

But George had a mind like a bear-trap with courage and determination to match. He was a widower. His wife of six years, a part-Crow woman, was buried under the big shaggy old cottonwoods inside the fancy iron fence a couple of hundred yards behind the log house where he lived.

When she had been alive, George had shaved every day, bathed twice a week, even in wintertime when folks don't sweat much, and changed his britches and shirt every three days. He'd continued to do those things for a year, maybe a year and a half, after her death, but nowadays he didn't look much different from his hired hands—excepting for Young Jim, who couldn't raise a decent set of stubble yet, being only eighteen and taffy-haired.

His foreman was Jeffrey Pelton, a dry, quiet, very capable rangeman who was just under forty and had enough of a dark look to him—black eyes and coarse black hair—to pass for a 'breed Indian, although he denied any such background.

George, Charley Wagner, and the *cosinero,* the ranch cook old Amos Butterfield who would only admit to sixty years, had most of the knowledgeability, but the youth and enduring toughness belonged to Jeff and Young Jim, something the older men tended to scoff at, because they were more experienced, and also because they were jealous.

Excepting Amos, who had spells of painful arthritis, or rheumatism, whatever it was, which affected his moods, the men at the Hinman place were predictable from day to day. They were also close-knit, more like a womanless family, or perhaps a horse-stealing and for-aging party of some Crow fraternity, than a chain of command. Charley, for instance, would argue himself blue in the face when he disagreed with some judgment George Hinman, his employer, or Jeff Pelton, his foreman, made. And the others would listen.

They were rangemen in the cattle business, first, employer and employees, second. The schoolma'm down in Kremmling would have called their association an epitome of democracy in action—and they would have stared woodenly and uncomprehendingly at her for saying such a thing. They were working cowmen dedicated to making a living and in the process fending off all the calamities from flash-floods to hung-up calves which only working cowmen knew very well afflicted an industry ignorant people thought of only in terms of natural freedom and horseback-riding.

The evening after Young Jim had been introduced to the pulled-calf, they sat in the cookshack discussing something else—three weeks without any rainfall—and Charley did not even mention what he and Young Jim had done that day. The hardest, often most unpleasant, work, was commonplace; rangemen did it, and thought ahead to whatever might be in the offing. It was largely a business of trying to anticipate difficulties. Like Charley had said, the things a man couldn't see, were all around him. The things he *could* see, well hell, he did whatever those things required of him.

They had been to the marking grounds a month earlier, in blustery, bitterly cold weather, and now all they had to do for as long as the bunch grass grew, was mind the cattle, and *that* at least, was part of the legend, because it was done a-horseback.

Amos told them about a horseless carriage he had seen when he'd gone down to Denver last month to visit his daughter and his son-in-law. He'd told them about it at least a dozen times since getting back home, but he did not tire of the subject, and the listening men at the supper table evidently did not tire of hearing about it.

Charley could not grasp the basics, though, and in an argumentative mood, he mentioned again, for the dozenth time, that it was ridiculous for folks to sit up in that contraption, while that liquid explosion was being squirted into a chamber where a little spark detonated it. Charley's contention was that if a man wanted to risk his life that way, it was his business, but he had no right at all to force his wife and children to sit up there with him, waiting to be blown to Kingdom Come. In fact, Charley was of the opinion that someone had ought to get up a law to protect women and children from being forced to undergo such coercion by dominating husbands and fathers.

George Hinman's view of the horseless carriage was that while it might get along tolerably well down in Denver, at least in the summertime, there was no possible future for anything like that in the countryside, and especially during Colorado's bitter, long cold winters.

George dismissed the horseless carriage as something people would play with, but which they would never take seriously, and with this judgment rendered, he mentioned something he'd heard from a rider who worked for the adjoining outfit, the MacDonald ranch.

'There is supposed to be a band of Crows in the north hills making meat, and that's something I haven't heard of in five, ten years.'

Charley was interested. 'How'd they get off the Reservation?'

Amos Butterfield looked disgustedly at Charley.

16

'Well now, how would you expect them to do it—they snuck away. How else could they manage it, with In'ian police and soljers, and lawmen, and just about everyone else, spying on 'em to make sure they stay where they belong.'

George said, 'Folks'll see the smoke and go up to look around. Then they'll race back to town and stir up a big ruckus about a band of scalp-hunters being loose.'

Jeff Pelton finished eating and thoughtfully sipped his coffee. 'How many are up there?' he asked. 'If it's a big band, it might be a good idea for folks not to go near the slopes.'

George had no idea how many Crows there were, but he doubted that it could be very many. 'Three, maybe four families,' he guessed. Then he raised tough eyes to the others. 'Not many still around now to make meat, let alone got the gumption to leave the Reservation and the government beef allotments, and strike out to do things the old way.'

Charley chewed and was thoughtful. Most rangemen, even the ones who did not like the Indians, respected the redskin way of life, probably because the rangeman's way was very similar. But Charley Wagner despised Indians. He sat and ate supper, drank coffee, listened to the others for a while, then ambled outside for a smoke on the veranda, and to watch the soaring moon when it passed above the rims.

No one heeded this. For one reason, smoking was not allowed in the cookshack. It was a ridiculous ruling, since old Amos not only smoked, himself, but also chewed snuff. Still, it was not allowed and George usually did not interfere in Amos's domain. Good cow-camp cooks were as scarce as teats on a bull.

Young Jim was interested in the Crows. In fact, he was fascinated, and the older men humored him, although, inevitably, they also began weaving improbable tales, too, which was how things were on a summer evening in just about any cow outfit between Lodgepole, Montana, and El Paso, Texas.

In the end, when they all drifted outside for a smoke, George made his judgment. 'No reason to go poking up there this early in the year, and by the time we push the cattle towards the hills—if they're really and truly up there—they'll have made their meat and be gone. Meanwhile, might be a good idea to just stay clear of the slopes—even the foothills. Just stay plumb away.'

Jeff was perfectly agreeable. From the doorway at their back Amos, fearful of not hearing everything which was being said and therefore ignoring his work to eavesdrop, put in his dollars worth.

'You bet your boots you'd best stay away from up there. Crows ain't Sioux, and ain't neither of 'em the Northern Cheyenne—now *there* was a fightin' In'ian— nevertheless, I can tell you something. Charley knows about this, too. Springtime, buck-In'ians rut just like bull-elks and boar-bears. Most other times of the year, they won't bother a man, but you get too close this time of year and—.'

'Oh hell, Amos,' growled Jeff. 'Rutting season was two months back. This here is summertime, damn it all, not springtime.'

Amos was stung, not by the contradiction but by the

derision, and his voice rose shrilly. 'All right. You smart-aleck, go on up there in broad daylight and hunt up the camp. They'll slit your pouch and yank your leg through it.' He glared at Jeff Pelton. 'What d'you young folks know? Go ask Charley. Ask George, there. Worst time of year to mess with redskins is in the spring-time—and the early summer too. Hmph!'

Amos stamped back to his dishpan, angry as a hornet, while Jeff turned a slow look towards his employer. George winked and crookedly grinned, but he also said, 'In a way he's plumb right. Of course that was a long time ago. But even the Crows, who are usually a friendly, generous people, can be dangerous in spring-time.'

'It's summer,' stated Jeff again, and killed the butt of his cigarette, looked over where Young Jim was standing, and said, 'Might be a good idea, before you turned in, to put an armload of kindling into Amos's woodbox.'

Young Jim departed and Jeff turned towards his employer. 'He was awful quiet this evening, George.'

Hinman chuckled. 'They pulled a calf today. Charley told me in the barn. Young Jim looked kind of peaked.'

Jeff was placated. 'I wondered what it was.' He smiled a little at the humor of the situation, then shrugged rangy shoulders. 'Well, Charley'll teach him. I wouldn't be surprised if someday Charley didn't find out his name, too.'

George eased down upon the porch railing gazing out where the yellow lamplight tumbled into the yard from a bunkhouse front window. 'I guess there's a lot of them,' he said softly. 'Runaways, abandoned, orphaned.' He faced Jeff. 'When I found him in an alley out back of Blackman's saloon he looked skin and bones, sore-eyed and tucked up like a gutted snowbird. He's come right along, Jeff, don't you figure?'

'Going to be big and strong as a bear, in a couple of years, too,' agreed Pelton. 'He's even learning to smile a little. That's usually a good sign.'

George yawned. 'What the hell kind of a man would do that to his own kin; abandon them?'

'Maybe he was an orphan. Maybe he just upped and run off, George.'

Hinman shook his head. 'I don't think so.' George did not give his reasons for saying this, he instead pushed up off the railing, sighed and looked around for the last time this particular night, then said, 'See you in the morning,' and went inside.

Jeff ambled down to the bunkhouse. The last one to get down there would be Young Jim, the only 'man' on the Hinman place who didn't own a last name; who didn't use one, anyway. He'd be along as soon as he finished filling Amos's wood-box.

Chapter Three
THE WOLF DEN

Something Young Jim had learned the previous year, when he'd had a sore behind and aching legs from too much horse-backing, was that livestockmen, while they were fond of horses and were proud of horsemanship, basically considered a horse's four long legs as an extenuation of their much shorter, two legs.

They could not possibly have operated over the rugged, endless miles without *some* kind of substitute for their own limited ability to get over the ground.

But they also carried this further. Horsemanship was a valuable possession and took longer to learn than cowmanship.

Jeff was probably the best horseman on the Hinman place, although Charley would have challenged that. It was Jeff who, in the evenings last summer, had taught Young Jim to name all the parts of a saddle, to distinguish between the different kind of riding bits, how to correctly saddle up and bridle his animals; not just do it the cowboy-way, but how to do it correctly—the horseman's way.

Young Jim, a year later, was perfectly at home with horses and their gear, although he would still be learning for another ten or fifteen years. He was becoming a passable roper too, but he and Charley argued about that. Charley tied hard and fast, Jeff had taught Young Jim to dally.

The day after pulling the calf they were on the north range looking for a wolf den George had reason to believe was up there, in a little spit of trees among some tawny old big rocks. No one killed wolves any more just because they were wolves, and in fact neither Charley nor Young Jim had a gun along. Young Jim did not own a gun and Charley's shellbelt and Colt hung from a wooden peg over his bunk gathering dust. Sometimes, when he went down to Kremmling, he buckled on the gun, but mostly, men no longer did that unless they had a valid reason. Charley's reason was simply that he had been doing it for more years than Young Jim was old, so he continued to do it. Times were changing, though; sometimes Charley Wagner would be the only armed rangerider in Blackman's saloon.

They had all day to locate the wolf's den and chase her back up to the mountains. No one wanted a bitch-wolf around, especially during calving time, when she had whelped nearby and couldn't range far enough from her den for wild game.

Usually, all it took to discourage a wolf was the scent of a man having passed within a half mile of the den. This time that probably would have been sufficient, but when Charley saw a hole with flies buzzing near its entrance and dismounted—his first mistake—to peer inside, the smell told him all he had to know. He reared back and called for Young Jim, who was still riding among the rocks, gingerly, also searching.

The yell may have done it, or perhaps the bitch inside her hole had caught Charley's scent, but whatever it was, she had four pups and the man-thing was outside, was blocking her way of escape. She could not be frightened off. It was too late for that, and she would not abandon her whelps. Also, she happened to be a fighting wolf, of which there were never very many, actually, but with her pups endangered, she came out of the hole like a thin, gray patchwork of shedding hair and flaming yellow eyes.

Charley heard the noise and looked down, barely in time. She slashed at his right leg with powerful, sharp teeth, tore his trousers but did not break the skin, and

22

Charley let go with a bawl of pure astonishment, aimed a wild kick, then turned to run for his horse, swearing at the top of his voice, the bitch-wolf coming after him without making a sound but with death in her eyes, and also in her heart.

Charley could not make it. He reached the horse, but the animal had already caught the wolf's rank scent and was doing his utmost to break free and race for home.

Charley turned and aimed another wild kick. This time, as the bitch paused to spring, a boot-toe knocked her off-balance and she missed, striking the horse's side, falling back to earth, righting herself frantically, and jumping clear to settle into the crouch again.

A rope sailed high, soundlessly, settled around the astounded wolf's neck, and Young Jim turned his panicky horse with his left hand, took his dallies with his right hand, sank in the spurs, and the bitch was yanked a foot into the air and dragged forty feet as the horse raced out of the rocks and trees.

Young Jim's intention was to drag the wolf to death. It did not work for him any better than it had worked for most other men who had tried it. Once the bitch could regain her feet, she avoided the one fatal mistake most roped animals made—she did not rear back to fight the rope, and get choked to death in the process. Instead, she loped along behind Young Jim's horse with plenty of slack in the rope to allow her to breathe normally.

Young Jim dug the horse harder. He was borne along in a wild, belly-down run. The bitch-wolf widened her stride and almost effortlessly kept up with the slack in the rope.

Regardless of how fast the horse ran—and he was a cowhorse, not a racehorse—the wolf ran just as fast. She eventually closed the distance and was loping alongside the horse. Young Jim was helpless. They had covered about four miles when he decided the only thing to do was cast off, so he let his dallies slip away, the rope fell into the grass, and this, finally, was the bitch-wolf's downfall. She ran into a snarl of rope, got her legs caught, and went end over end. Where she landed on her head and back, the grass barely covered a shale-stone ledge. She was knocked senseless.

Young Jim thought she had broken her neck and rode cautiously back for a closer look, and to retrieve his rope if he could. He dismounted, went in gingerly, loosened the rope, pulled it off, then saw the wolf's belly where the milk glands were, and understood instinctively why she had attacked. She had pups back in among the rocks.

He saw her rib-cage rise and fall, shallowly, felt her neck to be sure it wasn't broken, then coiled his rope, mounted up and headed back to Charley.

His horse was wringing wet, but by the time he got back to the rocks it had regained its wind. Charley, though, hadn't recovered. He was examining his torn trouser-leg when Young Jim rode on in, and straightened up to say fiercely, 'You killed the son of a bitch?'

Young Jim dismounted and loosened his cinch before tying his horse in cool tree-shade. 'No. She's got young.'

Charley blinked. 'Of course she's got young. Why'n hell do you expect she attacked me like that?' He turned and pointed. 'They're in that danged hole.' He scowled. 'Wasn't there no stick nor rock, or anything, to kill her with?'

Young Jim turned away from his horse toward Charley. 'I didn't look for none. I cast loose, she got tangled in the rope, went end over end and got knocked senseless in the shale when she hit her head. So I came back.'

Charley was stunned. 'She—you mean she was just *lyin'* there, unconscious, and you come back?'

'Yes.'

'For Cris'zake, boy, you could have killed her with your pocket-knife, if she was just lying there.'

'I could have,' stated Young Jim, one hand draped across his saddle-seat. 'Then what would happen to the pups?'

Charley couldn't speak for a moment. His face was almost scarlet, and it did not help any that Young Jim was standing over there as calm as stone. Finally, he said, 'Why, that old bitch was fixing to kill me, if she could. She was fixing to pounce me, boy, and once one of them gets a man flat on his back . . .' He stopped talking, let all his breath out audibly, then pulled down a fresh breath, and loosened a little at a time, until he was slouching where he stood, still staring at Young Jim. 'All right,' he said, curtly. 'All right. Let's get on back.'

They rode away, back out into the bright sunshine, without speaking for a long time. In fact, they had the log buildings in sight again, before either of them uttered a word. Charley's tough, bronzed face was closed down in an expression of unyielding indignation.

Young Jim said, 'Charley; if I'd been tied hard and fast to her, I couldn't have shucked loose of her, and then I don't know what would have happened. She wasn't even running hard, but she could stay up even with this horse.'

The advantages of dallying as opposed to tying hard and fast did not, at this moment anyway, seem at all pertinent to Charley Wagner. He turned his flinty face.

'There is the bitch,' he said. 'And likely she's got four or five pups in the den. Now that'll make five or six wolves prowling Hinman range next year at calving time. Young Jim, they can kill ten calves in one night. Boy, there ain't no excuse for lettin' that old bitch live. No excuse at all. And tomorrow, as soon as it's light, I'll go back up there—alone—with my sixgun, and take care of her and her blasted pups!'

They reached the yard out front of the barn just as dusk began settling in. Jeff was out back at a corral and came ambling through the barn to see them dismount. He stopped, stared at Charley's torn trousers, stared at Charley's bleak face, then went on over to the tie-rack to ask what had happened.

Charley told him, bitterly and angrily, while Young Jim, looking as miserable as he felt, tugged his saddle-animal on into the barn to off-saddle.

Charley left his horse at the rack and stamped furiously in the direction of the bunkhouse to put on his only other pair of britches, while Jeff walked on back down into the barn and watched Young Jim brush and comb his horse before turning it out. Finally, Jeff spoke.

'When they come out of the mountains, Young Jim, you got to scare them back, and if they den-up down here—well—then you got to kill 'em.'

Young Jim said nothing. He finished cuffing the horse and led it out back to the corral. Afterwards, he forked it some feed, and when he returned to the barn, Jeff was waiting. They looked at one another.

Young Jim said, 'I didn't want to make Charley mad at me.'

Jeff, gazing at the somber, youthful face, felt something for the boy he could not have defined. He smiled a little. 'Oh hell, he'll get over it. Anyway, he's not your only friend.'

'He's my best friend, Jeff.'

That same indefinable feeling assailed Jeff Pelton again. This time it left him floundering. He knew there was something to be said at this moment, but he had no idea at all what it was.

Then the youth made a remark that Jeff *could* respond to. He said, 'Jeff; I'm not sure I belong here. I never let Charley know yesterday, but pulling that calf—I almost got sick at my stomach.'

Jeff's smile returned, full of confidence. 'You belong, Young Jim. Take my word for it, you're a stockman. I did worse, the first time I helped pull a calf. I *did* get sick at my belly.'

'I don't want him to kill the mother-wolf and her pups, Jeff. I don't think I'm tough enough for—.'

'He's not going to kill 'em, Young Jim.'

'He said he'd ride back up there tomorrow with his sixgun and kill them all.'

'Naw,' scoffed Jeff Pelton. 'He can't do it and he knows damned well he can't do it.'

'Why?' asked the bewildered youth.

'Because, right now, that old bitch is packing her babies away in her teeth, one at a time. By the morning that den'll be cold and she'll be miles away. Maybe back in the mountains where she belongs. Charley knows that. He just said that because he was mad.'

Gradually, Young Jim relaxed his stance. 'I'm glad,' he exclaimed. 'I'll tell you why, Jeff. My paw used to beat my maw.'

The rangeboss stood stone still. This was the first time in over two years Young Jim had ever spoken about his past or his family.

'He'd get a look on his face—then he'd beat her. Couple times I tried to stop him. You see this little scar on my forehead? He wore a big gold ring. That's the scar it made the last time he hit me. And my mother turned on him that time. You got no right to kill the bitch-wolf for doing what she did, Jeff.'

Pelton nodded his head slowly. 'Young Jim, don't keep thinking about it. No one's going to kill her. Not this time anyway, and if she got scairt bad enough, she won't come out onto the grassland to den-up again. They're smart, son. They're *damned* smart. Now come along, let's get washed up for supper.'

Charley was out front in his other pair of trousers untying his horse from the rack. He looked up and Jeff Pelton scowled blackly at him, then herded Young Jim on over in the direction of the bunkhouse.

Charley watched, swore under his breath, then told his

28

horse Jeff was going to ruin that boy as sure as gawd made green apples, and walked the horse on down inside the barn.

Chapter Four
FRESH SIGN

Jeff talked for a while with George Hinman that evening after supper, out front of the main-house, then they sauntered down to the bunkhouse and talked with Charley Wagner in the bland night, and the following morning when Charley rode out, he had Young Jim with him, heading across the east range, and he did not mention the wolves. In fact, he never mentioned them again to Young Jim, and as they loped over the sun-bright, warm and fragrant range that following morning, Charley was his old self again, displaying nothing which would indicate how angry he had been the previous day.

At first, Young Jim was warily doubtful, then he turned hopeful, and finally, he smiled. After that, they rode along as though nothing had happened between them.

The purpose of their presence on the east range, which would not be used until late summer, was to make certain the salt-logs were in place and the waterholes were not too full of silt. Charley said this kind of work was absolutely contrary to the cowboy-legend, and laughed over that. They had two short-handled shovels along, and at the first sump hole, when they had to wade in and muck out the silt around the water vein, he said it was a shame some of those fellers who painted pictures of cowboys riding into the sunset had never worked the ranges, or they'd have had some different kinds of paintings to show.

There were three of those sump-springs to be cleaned, and by the time they had dug out the last one, and rode off, shovels over their shoulders like carelessly-carried rifles, they were sweaty, muddy, and hungry.

They made a miles-deep sweep northward, then along the grassland westerly a couple of miles out from the foothills to find the salt logs. This was a chore they could do without dismounting or using their shovels. A salt log was simply a length of tree-trunk, sometimes as long as fifteen feet, whittled out in the centre to a depth of about a foot, to nearly its full length, which made a big, heavy trough. In the grazing season these logs were filled with rock-salt, something the cattle craved, something their systems required, and salt-logs also had another value. Cattle would return to the area of the salt-logs almost daily. When a cowman wanted to check on his critters, he usually did not have to spend days hunting them on a miles-deep range, he simply had to ride to the salt-logs and wait a bit. The cattle would come straggling in for salt and he could sit his saddle at a discreet distance and make his inspection.

Two of the logs had no salt left in them, but the third one, which was only about a mile south of the foothills, had a solid chunk of salt its full length, unused from the previous year, and soaked through by winter snows and rain, until it had congealed into one long, solid block. Deer and elk, and an endless variety of smaller varmints such as porcupines, raccoons, pack-rats and even magpies, had left their marks in the salt-lick, and also on the ground around the log, but what stopped Charley and Young Jim in their tracks when they got over there, were chippings of hard salt upon the ground around the log, and the clear imprints of moccasins.

Charley's hair rose along the back of his neck as he stiffened in his saddle and turned to look in all directions. The moccasin imprints were fresh, and out a short distance there were also fresh marks made by unshod horses' hooves.

'Gawddamned In'ians,' Charley said softly, running a long look in the direction of the foothills, last, and watching that direction all the time he was speaking. 'Those are fresh tracks. Not even no dew been on them. Those devils been down here this morning. Maybe they saw us coming and went back, but anyway, they was here not more'n an hour or two ago.'

It may have been true and it probably was true, but there was no Indian in sight now. Young Jim, with younger and stronger eyes, searched intently, then said, 'They're gone, Charley. What did they break up the salt for?'

'In'ians need it just like everyone else,' replied the older man, turning back, finally, to considering the log. 'Specially when they're making meat.'

Young Jim, having heard this term before without understanding it, asked what 'making meat' meant. Charley looked over his shoulder before answering, then he shoved back his hat, clasped both hands atop his saddlehorn with the shovel, like a rifle, lying across his lap, and answered.

'They kill big game—elk and the like—render out all the meat fit to eat, pull out the entrails and lay them out flat in a long line, then punch out all the undigested stuff in each gut, turn the entrails inside out, wash 'em good in a creek, turn 'em back outside in again, tie off the end, and cook up a lot of meat, flavor it with herbs—and salt—and other stuff, pound it into a sort of mash, then stuff the guts with it. I've seen guts full of that meat ten, fifteen feet long. It keeps all winter. They also skive meat with the grain, so thin it'll dry hard, like boot-leather, then salt it and pepper it, and sprinkle their damned herbs over it, and dry it on racks in the sun—jerky.' Charley finished by looking at the youth and saying, 'That's making meat. Now let's get the hell on back. The fellers can quit wondering if they got In'ians in our mountains.'

As they turned southward from the area of the salt-log, Young Jim eyed Charley Wagner thoughtfully. 'How is it that you know so much about Indians?' he asked, and Charley's face was momentarily seized by a spasm of emotion, then it was gone and he framed his response.

'I been around a long while, Young Jim. But it hasn't been too long when there was a lot more of 'em than there is now, and a man'd run onto them every now and then. And like I told you, I wintered a time or two with In'ians.'

'You don't like them, do you, Charley?'

This time the response came more slowly, and only

after Charley had covered a dozen or so yards. 'A preacher told me one time folks don't like what's different from 'em, son. In'ians are different.'

The look on the older man's face warned Young Jim to let go of this topic, so he branched off a little. 'Back home one time I found a magazine in a trash-can out back of a store with stories in it about the Indians. It said they were the best horsethieves in the world.'

Charley turned indignantly. 'Well now, hell boy, that's sure some distinction, isn't it? There's nothing lower than a horsethief. That's fine stuff to be putting into magazines for youngsters to read, is all I got to say.'

Young Jim almost smiled at his companion's quick disgust, but he controlled the urge and offered a placating comment. 'The magazine didn't say horsethieves were decent folks, Charley. It just said Indians were better at it than anyone else.'

Charley scowled and pursed his lips in hard thought, then eventually said, 'No sir, I don't agree with that. If you want a real shrewd horsethief, go find yourself a Messican. They're better at it because they're better horsemen. They don't run off *all* a man's horses, they pick and choose. And they don't ride horses to death like In'ians do. Messicans are good horsemen; they take care of their animals. Nope, son, I'd say a Messican makes the best horsethief.'

'What *are* Indians good at then, Charley?' asked Young Jim, and instantly saw that he had made a mistake. The expression that returned to Charley's face was bitter and cruel again.

'Making meat,' answered the older man, curtly, and

33

booted out his horse into a handy lope.

They did not reach the ranch yard until sundown. They hadn't ridden fast, and in any case, Hinman-range was vastly extensive.

Amos was sitting in shade over alongside the cook-shack plucking a freshly killed sage hen. He had three more to pluck. Jeff and George were over on the bunkhouse porch, having returned from the south range, down among the cattle, only a short while earlier. They waved as Young Jim and Charley walked their mounts on in. Jeff grinned. 'They been mucking out, all right,' he said, referring to the caked mud on the riders' clothing. 'Charley'll have to do his laundry tomorrow, now. That's his only other pair of britches.'

George had passed over the sweaty, dirty appearance, and had noticed something else. 'They got along well today,' he observed. 'Young Jim don't have that closed-in look, now.'

Amos called towards the dismounting men. 'Hey, Young Jim, you could come help me pluck these danged birds when you're through down there, if you was of a mind to.'

Charley glowered, 'The lad's put in his day, Amos.'

On the porch, George groaned. Now, rebuffed Amos would sulk. George shook his head. 'We got more damned temperment out here,' he told his rangeboss, 'than a man can shake a stick at.'

Jeff smiled. 'It was you shot the sage hens, George. Otherwise, Amos'd be inside making stew.'

Charley and Young Jim put their shovels in the tool-house, which also happened to be the shoeing-shed,

34

then sauntered to the bunkhouse porch to report on what they had done. The last thing Charley reported, was the fresh redskin sign at the last salt-log.

George and Jeff stared at him. 'How fresh?' asked Jeff.

'No more'n an hour or two before Young Jim and me rode up,' replied Charley. 'And my guess is that they saw us and humped their backs getting back up-country. They'll be back. The log's still a third full of salt. They'll clean it down to the bottom.'

George asked how many, and Charley looked pained. 'I'm no tracker. Never was that good at reading sign, either. You want me to guess?'

'Yes.'

'Six or eight of 'em; big marks—four or five of 'em—made by bucks, the other smaller tracks made by squaws. Unshod horses, and in the salt, marks where someone had used a knife and a hatchet to break up the pieces.'

George began thoughtfully rolling a smoke with the others watching, and when Jeff Pelton said, 'You got to have salt to make meat,' Young Jim looked at him, not expecting the second-youngest man among them to know about making meat.

George lit up and blew smoke. 'Yeah. The sooner they get it all the sooner they'll get back up there where they belong.' He looked around. 'No sense in making something big out of this—like telling anyone we run across. They'll be up there a couple of months, then they'll move.'

Charley had a question. 'Where'll they move to? If

they're on the run, with maybe the army looking for 'em, they'll likely stay right where they are.'

Young Jim spoke up. 'The army could track them down.'

All three of the older men got busy examining their boots or their fingernails, or in George Hinman's case, the burning tip of his smoke.

Charley quietly said, 'No one's going to track them down, Young Jim. They ain't the first reservation-jumpers. You don't track no In'ian down if he don't want you to. They'll have brushed out their tracks for ten miles before they got into Hinman hills.'

Young Jim reddened, and afterwards listened, but did not speak again.

Jeff Pelton sighed, glanced over where old Amos was furiously plucking his birds, and shoved up out of the chair. 'I'll go help Amos,' he grumbled. 'We're not going to get fed until someone does.' As he walked off Young Jim also arose and turned to look over there, then he too volunteered to go help the *cosinero,* which left Charley and George, the two oldest men, upon the bunkhouse porch. Charley took the chair Jeff had vacated, swung his tired legs to the railing, cocked his muddy boots up there, and garrulously said, 'That's a right good boy, and in a couple of years he'll be as good a rangerider as you ever had, George. But—there's an odd streak in him about fightin' and the like.'

'We explained that to you last night,' stated Hinman. 'Jeff told you what he said about his paw taking after his maw, and how she tried to protect the lad once.'

Charley accepted that. 'Yeah, I know. And I understand. But the thing is, a man can't always turn his back on things that ought to be done, George, and you damned well know that, no matter how unpleasant they are.'

Hinman was slower responding this time. He knew Charley was correct, but he leaned strongly in favor of Young Jim, too, and that conflict kept him quiet until they both heard old Amos raise his voice in petulant disgust about the way his helpers were plucking the sage hens, and this offered George a way out of his dilemma, by turning away from it entirely, by changing the subject.

He said, 'Well hell, the lad's sure going to learn one thing outside cow-camp work, that all folks aren't the same. If he can live with old Amos, when the arthritis is bothering him, he'd ought to be able to learn to live with anyone.'

Charley, who felt strongly about Amos's periods of temperament, agreed wholeheartedly. 'Lord, yes. You never said truer words.' He slapped his legs, shot up to his feet and turned away. 'I got to clean up,' he said, and walked off leaving George alone in the quiet, bland evening.

Chapter Five
RIDING NORTH

Amos had a long list for George the following morning. George had business to tend to in Kremmling anyway, and no working cowman just upped and loped off to town on a single errand, they waited until there were a number of things to be done, then spent a full day doing them all so that they would not have to visit town too often. Not that most of them did not like going to town, but they liked better remaining on their ranges. Town meant wearing clean britches, rubbing hub-grease into a man's boots, and even sometimes having one of the other men do some hair shearing.

George had the team on the light spring-wagon before his hired hands trooped out of the cookshack from breakfast and saw him down at the tie-rack, working. But Amos had already told them he'd be going to town today, so they'd had time to ponder over their requirements, which consisted mainly of a bottle of whisky or two, a dozen sacks of tobacco, and in Charley's case, a new set of britches.

They wrote it all down and gave it to George. The only one who hadn't listed anything was Young Jim. George noticed this but said nothing about it. He told Jeff two men had ought to go south and look at springing heifers and one man had ought to go northeast and mark trees.

Since looking at the heifers implied pulling hung-up calves, Young Jim instantly volunteered to go tree-marking. The older men gazed at him stone-faced, restraining an urge to break into laughter. George and Jeff gravely nodded and Young Jim went to the shed for a hatchet. After he was gone, Charley said, 'Nevertheless, it wouldn't do him no harm, getting at it first-hand.'

Jeff shrugged that away. 'Plenty of time, Charley.'

George climbed to the spring-seat, clucked up his

team and went jouncing out of the yard on a southeasterly course. Charley and Jeff went out back to catch horses and lead them inside to rig out. Young Jim also caught a horse, but the older men were almost finished when he led his animal in to be bridled and saddled. As they led their horses outside to be mounted—there was a cardinal rule on every cow-outfit against mounting a fresh horse inside a barn—Charley looked back and said, 'Try to blaze the ones nearest flat country, will you, son?'

Young Jim agreed, and as the older men rode off, he did as he had been taught to do; he led his horse outside and turned it completely around twice, before mounting it and heading northwesterly, alone, with the hatchet-handle sticking up behind the cantle.

Marking trees was a little like making meat. In the easy time between marking and turning the cattle out, and rounding them up in the autumn and working them again, the less essential but other important chores were taken care of. Marking trees meant someone rode up along the foothills with an axe, cut a clean mark—a blaze—on the trees best suited for firewood, counted them, then returned to the ranch, and when they could take the time, everyone went forth with cross-cut saws and axes, riding a couple of wagons stripped down to the running-gear, the trees were felled, loaded upon the running-gears, and hauled back to the ranch for cutting into firewood-size later, usually in the evenings after the work-day was finished. It took many cords of wood to keep a cow-outfit warm through the long Colorado winters.

Young Jim had blazed trees with George his first summer, a couple of years back. Last year, he and Jeff had ridden out to mark the wood. This year he was going out alone, and it pleased him. He never shirked responsibility, which was something the older men had watched him for, and had complimented themselves about discovering in him, when they had finally found it. A man who couldn't see what had to be done, and do it without awaiting instructions, was useless.

There were some clouds with soiled edges over the northeasterly peaks, which was the direction from which most summer rainstorms came. They needed rain badly. The grass was heading out already, which meant it would stop growing tall unless it got moisture. Young Jim rode through the sultry sunshine studying those clouds and trying to do as Charley did; guess how much water might be in them, and how long it would take for them to get down across Hinman-range and open up. He grinned to himself about that. He felt more like a professional today than he had felt before. Other times they had entrusted him to do things by himself, but they had been routine jobs, like running in the saddle-stock or chousing bulls out of the mudholes and back to where the cows were. This time, it would be his judgment alone which determined which trees were best for making wood. This time, he would function as a seasoned stockman.

It was a long ride so he booted out his animal and held him to an easy lope for several miles, free as a bird in a greeny world which had no real limits, and whose mountain-perimeters were really only challenges. He

40

saw larks in the rank grass and heard some crows raucously crying warnings when he loped past a clutch of trees.

When he hauled back down to a walk, he thought of Jeff and Charley, and with a small sense of guilt about deliberately avoiding going south with one of them, told his horse aloud that one of these days he'd do it—he'd get down on his knees exactly as Charley had done, and pull a hung-up calf. He could remember every detail of that experience very vividly, which seemed to be the way with things a man would just as soon not remember; at least would just as soon not remember quite so vividly.

By the time the sun was almost to its meridian, and a horseman's shadow upon the grass had steadily shrunk down until, as it kept rocking pace beside him, it resembled a distorted, midget-like blob, Young Jim could see individual trees along the foremost forest-ranks well enough to turn selective.

The actual mountain was a mile farther back. Where the grassland ended and the foremost trees stood in their stair-stepped tiers, were flat to rolling foothills. Here, which was all country accessible to wheeled vehicles, was where he would make his blazes. It was hard enough work felling those immense pines and firs, and limbing them, and loading them onto the running-gears, without having to also trundle the trimmed trunks on rollers any distance to reach the wagons. With this kind of hard work, as with any kind, if a man didn't use his head every way he could, his back and arms and legs had to pay for it.

Charley would be critical, and that was also in Young Jim's mind. George and Jeff would look and say nothing, when Young Jim made a mistake. Unless it was too glaring a one. But Charley would speak up right away.

He finally was within the fragrance of the great trees, with excited birds scolding him from on high. There was a small creek coming on a crooked course down out of the perpetual gloom of the farther slopes and forests, where Young Jim tanked up, then watered his horse, and afterwards lay back for a while upon warm earth watching those steadily oncoming cloud-shapes. They resembled a flotilla of ghostly galleons of the kind he had seen once in a calendar-picture, pennants flying, proud bows lifting and sinking, rank after rank of them, with soiled edges to the billows where the sails were.

A big fat marmot came through the grass, saw him, reared up, turned its head away and beadily eyed him with only its right eye, acting more curious than fearful. He talked to it, warned it against his kind, told it he had been informed that it was a stupid animal, and finally, when he pushed it upright out of the grass to walk on again, the marmot fled, but not very fast because it was too fat for swiftness.

Young Jim took loose his axe and strolled along leading the horse, studying trees with the air of a field marshal critically inspecting troops. He hacked in a blaze upon a magnificent old forest monarch, a bull-pine with limbs its full length and a shaggy, unkempt look. It had just about reached its full life-span.

Within another few years insidious rot would begin destroying it.

He did not select trees which would shortly begin to deteriorate because he knew this to be the case. He actually knew almost nothing about trees, beyond the fact that when the wood had dried all summer it burned well on snowy, windy nights. The reason he selected one big bull-pine after another, until he came across some big old red-firs, was because they had more wood in them than younger trees had.

Each running-gear would hold three monarchs or five younger and smaller trees. Young Jim marked only monarchs. If George or Jeff wanted to make a change, they could do so when they got up here.

It only took a couple of hours to make the careful selection. He had chosen only large trees, and only those which were adjacent to flat land. When the job was finished he retraced his steps as far as that little cold-water creek, making certain he had picked the best trees.

He had. At least, for the purpose, he had, and he told the horse he would bet a day's work neither George nor Jeff would change a single blaze.

It was past noon, but not very far past. He had brought no food, but then he had long ago abandoned the habit of eating in the middle of the day. Like many rangeriders who were never anywhere near a cookshack when mid-day arrived, Young Jim's two daily meals— breakfast and supper—adequately compensated for the missed mid-day meal.

His horse tugged on the reins at the creek, so they

drank again, and because this was such a warm and pleasant place, he allowed the horse to drag his reins and graze while Young Jim, still with the axe in hand, sank down in the grass with the soporific sound of that little hurrying creek at his back.

He looked southward over an immensity of land that made him feel smaller than a flea. Those clouds were finally bearing down, adding something to the hush and heavy humidity. Behind him, on his left up through the trees somewhere, an animal snuffled and Young Jim whirled with hair rising along the back of his neck. Bull elks would fight a man in rutting season, even a mounted man. But rutting season was over.

Still, the older men had warned him. Never crowd any big animal, no matter what time of year it was, and bears least of all.

He arose, thinking now in terms of a boar-bear. With only the hand-axe, as a weapon, he turned to sidle towards the distant grazing horse.

The sound came again. This time his fear faded a little because it sounded like a horse, up through the trees. He turned to look back where his animal was grazing. The horse had evidently not heard that first sound, but he'd heard the second sound because he was standing utterly motionless, legs spread, head down, ears up and pointing while he sampled the scents coming southward out of the trees. The horse nickered, and instantly there was an answering nicker from up through the trees, accompanied by what sounded to Young Jim like the exasperated pawing of a tethered horse.

The thought which entered Young Jim's mind was not

the thought which would have entered Charley Wagner's mind. Charley would have thought a tethered horse up through the trees belonged to a skulking Indian. Young Jim thought the horse was probably snagged in bushes or vines and could not get free, so he started on up into the forest, still carrying the hand-axe.

Behind him, his saddled mount also became curious and began heading into the trees. Charley would have noticed something else; there were no birds. Ordinarily a forest-fringe had birds in every treetop. This time, there was not even a scolding bluejay, but Young Jim did not notice anything like that. He had been in the range-country going on three years; the previous fifteen he had never been out of sight of the cobblestone roads nor brick store-fronts. He had become a good rider and was on his way to also becoming a good stockman—but even most youths his age who had been born and reared in cow-country, had no reason to learn the things their fathers and grandfathers had had to learn well to stay alive, such as reading some significance into totally empty and silent treetops, when there should have been birds up there.

He plowed straight on up into the dusk-gloom of the scented forest following along the little crooked water-course, and saw the horse, finally. It was not trapped in vines, it was tied by a rope rein, and nearby upon the ground in blankets looking ill and covered with sweat, was a girl with golden-toned skin, liquid large very dark eyes, and two plaits of ebon hair. Around her were blankets, some mounded tree moss, a *parfleche* of food, and close to her outstretched right hand, a battered old long-

45

barreled dragoon revolver. She was biting her underlip and staring glassily at the tall, lanky youth in front of her, holding a naked axe in his fist.

Chapter Six
A SURPRISE FOR YOUNG JIM

Young Jim was too stunned to move, let alone speak. The girl's hand was reaching slowly for the old long-barreled pistol but her eyes never left his face. His horse, locating the Indian horse, walked on over to trade sniffs and toss its head.

The silence was deep and enduring.

Young Jim watched the girl's hand close around the pistol grips. He asked, 'Are you sick?'

She did not lift the gun, then, but neither did she relinquish her hold on it. Instead of answering, she said, 'Why do you have that axe?'

He looked down. The axe was hanging at his side, forgotten. 'That? Well, I've been marking trees so's we can come back later with wagons and cut them down for . . .'

He bit the words off and tossed the axe upon the spongy layer of pine needles underfoot. The girl did not take her hand off the horse-pistol but she seemed less than ever inclined to lift the thing.

He repeated his question. 'Are you sick, lady? You don't look very good.'

She answered flatly. 'I am shot.' Her very dark eyes were accusing. 'You have never been shot?'

He said, 'No,' then he frowned at her. 'What are you

46

doing here, if you have been hurt? Why aren't you with your folks?'

'They don't need another burden,' she replied, and rolled back part of the blanket to show an immense area of bluish flesh around her upper leg where a small hole showed with red moisture, and on the inside of her leg, there was a much larger, ripped-out, ragged wound, this latter hole as large as a silver dollar.

Young Jim's breath hung up for a second. 'You got to have care,' he told her. 'You need a doctor, lady.'

'I need this,' she said, indicating the creek, then the mounded tree-moss. 'I need to be left alone. It will heal, but it will be a long time.'

He sank down to his knees. Another time the sight of her two-thirds bare, golden legs would have affected him altogether differently, but the wound was a terrible thing to see, and it was all he saw, until she flipped the blanket back over it, covering her legs again.

'Why did they shoot you?' he blurted at her.

'It was at night when we were passing a settlement a long ways beyond the mountains. Dogs barked and men ran out with rifles.' She looked steadily at him. 'White men. They also shot an old man, but he died so we buried him.'

'You rode all this way with that hole in your leg?'

She nodded, and reached a hand into the creek-water with a balled-up cloth in it, then wiped her face. The old dragoon pistol lay in the grass again, close by her but no longer in her hand. 'Who will you tell?' she asked.

He sighed and rocked back on his haunches to meet her gaze and to guess her thoughts. 'No one, if you

47

don't want me to—but you should be carried out to a doctor. That hole could fester up and give you blood-poisoning.'

'I know what to do; it will be all right. But not for a long time, and I can't ride any more. If you bring back white men they will shoot me anyway.'

He stared at her. It was on the tip of his tongue to deny that what she said about George or Jeff or Charley shooting her was true, then he remembered the tough, casual way they had talked of the Indians, and simply hunkered there looking at her.

She was beautiful, perhaps his own age or a year or two older, and although she had to have a fever and be in pain, her expression was stonily serene—fatalistic, but Young Jim did not know the word nor its meaning.

He pointed to the *parfleche* pouch. 'Food?'

'Yes.'

He eyed the bag skeptically. 'It's not very much, is it?'

'I can make it last.'

He changed position and sat down flat upon the soft forest floor, tossed aside his hat and looked over where the horses were, then looked back shaking his head. 'You can't make it alone, lady. Suppose you go out of your head; suppose a bear or some varmint finds you? If you can't walk, how can you graze the horse?'

She said nothing.

He plucked some grass, chewed it, looked elsewhere, then threw up his hands. 'If you'd let me, I could rig up something between the two horses, and walk you down out of here to—.'

'No!'

He spat out the grass, met her tawny gaze and said, 'All right. But you're sure pig-headed. But all right; I'll go down to the ranch, get some medicine, some grub and some blankets and come back.'

'And bring others,' she accused him.

Young Jim rarely swore, but he knew how it was done; anyone who had been three years among rangemen, knew how swearing was done. 'Damn it all,' he exclaimed, 'I told you before—I won't tell a soul.'

She studied his face a moment before speaking again. 'I'm a Crow, your enemy,' she told him.

'Lady, you're not my enemy. I don't figure I have any enemies. And we heard about a week back down at the ranch, there was In'ians in the mountains. My boss said we'd keep clear and maybe when you folks finished making meat you'd go away and that would be that.'

'How could you have known we were up here? No one has made smoke in the daytime. We have kept scouts out to make sure no one found us. How could you have known?'

Young Jim could not recall exactly how the subject had come up, now, but he knew it had so he said, 'There was talk, that's all. What difference does it make? If the Hinman-riders don't bother you, and you're on George Hinman's land, who could make you any trouble?' Having said this, Young Jim glanced at the axe, picked it up and put it over closer to her. 'You keep this. Maybe you can use it for something.' He started to rise, and smiled at her. 'Quit acting scairt. I'm not going to say a thing, and they won't know at the ranch when I've snuck away to come back.' He hung there a moment

49

longer before getting back upright. 'How long you been here beside the creek, anyway?'

'Two days.'

'And your folks haven't hunted you down in all that time?'

She looked skeptically at him. 'Don't you know how to drag out your sign?'

He didn't because he not only had never done it, but he had never been told how others did it. 'No ma'm.' He stood up with a sudden chilling thought coming to blot every other consideration. Suppose George or Jeff decided they should come up after the wood tomorrow or the next day? It was a reasonable assumption; aside from watching the drift, and minding springtime first-calf heifers, there was little else to do this time of year.

She said, 'What is it?'

He told her. Then they stared at one another for a moment until a solution came to him. 'I'll find out tonight if they figure to do that, and if they do, when I come back we'll move your camp back up the creek a couple of miles.' He smiled again, with relief this time, and with pride at having thought of the solution.

'You,' she told him solemnly, 'are going to get into trouble.'

He did not disavow such a possibility, but he was not thinking of it in the same terms that she was. 'Maybe just a little,' he admitted.

'For helping an Indian,' she told him, bitterly.

That had not been in his mind at all. He might get in trouble for stealing food from Amos's cookshack, and for slinking away on a ranch horse, and keeping their secret from the others, but the fact that she was a Crow did not enter his mind until she mentioned it, then he said, 'Not that; no.'

She mopped perspiration from her face again with the little balled-up rag, and cupped both hands to convey water to her mouth. She drank a lot of water, with Young Jim wondering why she hadn't brought along a cup. He stooped to retrieve his hat, dumped it upon the back of his head, and finally asked a question which, with someone else, would have come long ago.

'Lady; how come, for an In'ian, you speak English so good?'

She mopped her neck with the damp, cold rag. 'I was an orphan. They took me to the Sisters of Mercy school . . . I went home four years ago, and hid when they came to take us back again.' Her dark eyes flashed at him. 'I had a knife to kill myself with if they had found me.'

Instead of the recriminations she seemed to expect from him, she got an understanding nod. 'I know,' he told her. 'I wouldn't have used a knife, but when they looked for me, I was better at hiding than they were at hunting.'

A slight frown showed across her golden face. 'Why did they hunt you?'

'It don't matter now, lady, because they never caught me . . . I don't like to talk about it.' He straightened back. 'I'll head for home now. You need some wood for a fire or anything, before I go?'

'No . . . What is your name?'

'Young Jim.'

She accepted that. 'Young Jim . . . I am Elena.'

51

He repeated it. 'That's a pretty name. You'll be all right until I get back?'

'Yes.'

He went over, led his horse out and mounted it, then smiled down at her and rode across the dappled shadows in the direction of the yonder afternoon sunlight.

He had no idea how much time had passed, until he was loping southward and glanced at the cluttering-up sky with the rain-clouds closing in on all sides, permitting the sun to only show through in one place. It was late afternoon.

He urged the horse along to try and make up lost time, but by the time he had the ranch in sight, with the sun gone finally and those swollen clouds lowering ominously overhead, there was not much danger of anyone questioning the length of time he had spent up-country.

The others had returned earlier. The spring-wagon was parked beside the shoeing-shed, where it was kept, which meant that George had returned from town, too.

When he rode into the yard and dismounted in front of the barn, there was the sound of men's voices coming from the open bunkhouse door. There was a poker game in progress in there.

He cared for his animal, paused out front to study the sky again, and decided that if it rained tonight, there would be no one going after wood tomorrow, or, depending upon how long it rained, the day after either. Laden wagons sank into soft earth.

But it also posed another problem. He had decided, on the ride back, to wait until everyone was snoring, then load up and head back for Elena's camp. She did not have anything which was waterproof. There were ponchos and waxed tarps in the saddle-room. If there was one danger she should not court it was getting chilled, maybe catching pneumonia.

Riding back up there through a rainstorm would be unpleasant, but he shrugged that off and hiked over to the bunkhouse, where the men looked up as he entered, and Charley said, 'About time. We was beginning to figure you'd maybe got caught by a bear.'

George and Jeff smiled and turned back to the poker game. They were both losing to Charley.

Young Jim went out back to the wash-rack, cleaned up, then ambled over to the cookshack to see if he could help Amos—actually, to spy out where the things were kept he would want to take back with him.

Amos looked surprised, then pleased, when Young Jim walked in offering to lend a hand. 'Only man on the damned ranch,' he said, 'who'd lift a hand if I was to get down with a complaint. Well; you can commence by laying out the crockery and forks and such like.' Amos's mood changed drastically. 'Well; you find some decent trees today?'

'Yes . . . Amos, don't folks use quinine for fevers?'

The cook stared. 'Yes. You feel a fever coming on?'

'No. I was just wondering, is all . . . Do we have quinine on the ranch?'

Amos pointed. 'In that cupboard. That's where we keep all the medicine for everything from a man being bound up, to snake remedy . . . Say, are you figuring to be a doctor?'

'No, nothing like that. Do you want me to peel the potatoes?'

Amos's lined old face split wide. 'If you're a mind to, son. I'd take it right kindly. My rheumatism ain't too bad today, but with the rain coming it's bound to be a bother to me tomorrow. In that bin yonder. You'll find a peelin' knife in drawer aside the stove.' Amos leaned to peer at the sky beyond the nearest window. 'We're going to get it tonight, and the Lord knows we sure need it.'

Chapter Seven
RAIN

Young Jim was normally an early and sound sleeper. If his mind had been clear he undoubtedly would have slept like a log this night, too, because there was a warm wind yonder and the air had a heavy, good damp scent to it. It was the kind of a night when folks could sleep like stones.

The other men in the bunkhouse had been asleep for several hours. The night was utterly hushed, except for the occasional sounds that little wind made.

Young Jim rolled out silently, took his britches, shirt, hat and boots out to the yard, and dressed himself out there. He knew the feeling of furtiveness, but for the past couple of years and longer, he had not felt any need to be furtive. Still, something he had achieved a certain expertness in, years past, had not left him. He made it to the cookshack without trouble, got inside and started to make up a bundle. Even in the dark, he moved swiftly and unerringly. It did not take long. The last thing he appropriated was one of the graniteware metal cups. Then he went wraith-like down to the barn and rigged out a horse.

There were ponchos in the harness-room. He took one for Elena, but put it on himself for the ride north. He also took along a waterproof wagon-top, which was the heaviest article, besides himself, the horse had to carry. Then he rode out the back of the barn at a walk, watching behind for a light, perhaps, if they had discovered his absence at the bunkhouse, or possibly someone standing outside in his stocking-feet, looking around.

There was nothing. No one knew he had left the ranch. He settled forward, urged the horse along, and after a few miles he smiled to himself.

But of course it was no great accomplishment to deceive people who had no reason to believe they would be deceived.

The rain held off until he was more than two-thirds of the way towards the foothill-forest, and even when it finally began, although the raindrops were large, they were also few and far between.

He did not care much anyway, inside his black poncho, except that the sky, being low and completely filled in from horizon to horizon, blocked out even the little help starshine would have given him. It was like riding through the inside of a boot.

He knew the terrain, but even if he hadn't there was no danger, it was all open country, except for an infrequent stand of rocks which usually had a few trees growing among them.

The horse was large and powerful. He carried his overload handily. They made good time, partially because of the horse's strength and stamina, and partially because Young Jim knew exactly where he was going. By the time they reached the trees, though, those big fat raindrops were becoming heavier and thicker. They made a sound in the treetops like they made back at the ranch atop the bunkhouse.

Young Jim had no difficulty. He located the little creek, then dismounted beside it and tramped ahead leading the burdened horse. Because riders' ponchos were made longer than most raincoats, and with a more voluminous cut in order to also cover a man's saddle, Young Jim looked more like a great black bird than he did a man as he led the horse on in through the trees alongside the little creek.

It did not occur to him to sniff for cook-fire smoke, which he might not have been able to detect because of the increasing rainfall, but if it had been Charley Wagner the approach would have taken the detection of smoke into consideration. Also, Charley would not have come up unarmed. Young Jim had not even thought of weapons.

He saw the Indian horse first, still tied in the same place, and fretting as the rainfall increased. He did not see the Crow girl until he halted in the pitchblende-gloom and she moved a little, baring her head from the blanket she'd mounded up over herself until she resembled a dark stone.

He called lightly to her, then tied the horse and began

removing the pack. She said nothing, but watched everything he did.

First, he slung his lariat between two trees, then draped the waterproof canvas across it, stretched out the sides and pegged them down, using the hand-axe he'd left with her.

After that, he made two trips to the horse to bring in the supplies, and the last time, Elena had let the blanket fall to her waist, now that no rainfall touched her. Tawny dark eyes watched everything he did, and when he handed her the graniteware cup, she took it and smiled. He was stopped cold. She had not smiled before, at their other meeting. Without smiling, she was very handsome, *with* a smile she was beautiful, even under a soiled canvas in a damp-smelling forest, in almost total darkness.

He dug out medicines, the quinine first. 'This is supposed to help a fever,' he explained, then picked up a smaller, darker bottle. 'This stuff burns like the devil; I know, because I've had it daubed on me a few times. But it'll keep down infection. And this here is a clean dish-towel. You can cut it up into bandages . . . The rest of this stuff is tinned peaches and corn and peas, and such like.'

He leaned back on his haunches. There was very little head-room inside the improvised shelter. She looked a little better; that is, she could smile at him, and she did not seem as tense as she had that morning. He dumped his hat and sank lower, the old black poncho flowing out around him, shiny with wetness.

'No one saw you leave?' she asked.

'Nope. They were sleeping like a bunch of dead men. I figure this stuff'll take care of you for a couple of days. I'll fetch back more food, then.'

She said, 'They will miss the wagon-cover, won't they? Or the food?'

He did not think so. 'The tarp's been lying in the harness-room for a couple of years and we've never used it. The cookshack shelves are full of tinned peaches and the like.' He did not think of the medicine and evidently neither did she. Nor did they think of something else—the horse which would be ridden down by the time Young Jim turned it out in the early morning.

Their eyes held until she lowered hers when she told him he was taking chances he did not have to take. He answered very simply.

'Sure I had to take them. I know; you figure you can do it all by yourself, and maybe you can, but you can do it a lot easier and better with some help, and that's a fact.'

She did not argue with him, and when a little damp wind came under one side of the old canvas, she pulled the blanket closer when she raised her head and smiled again.

'We are friends, Young Jim.'

The brightness of her gaze made him uncomfortable, so he picked up his hat, then started to remove the poncho. She frowned. 'I don't need the rubber coat.'

'Sure you do,' he averred, and had it almost removed when she refused to take it.

'You'll need it on the ride back. Look; no water can come inside here, can it? Then why would I need the rubber coat. I won't take it.'

He sighed, shrugged back into the old poncho and pulled his hat down, hard. 'I got to get back, Elena, and you mind now, and take good care. Don't catch the pneumonia, and take that quinine if you feel feverish. And keep dry. I could make you a little fire in here, before I go, and bring in a few armloads of wood.'

She shook her head at him. 'I don't need a fire. It's wet, but it is not cold . . . Young Jim?' She held out a hand palm upward. He leaned to grasp her hand, and squeeze a little, then he smiled straight at her. 'You know how folks feel when they're alone? They get to feeling sorry for themselves. I know about that, too. Well; you're not alone.' He released her hand and backed out of the low shelter, waved once as he arose, then turned to go back and climb astraddle a cold, wet saddle-seat. He considered changing the Indian horse to another place, where it could pick a little grass, groaned down out of the wet saddle to do this, and the horse was ravenous from being tied so long with nothing to eat.

Finally, riding back down towards the open range, he looked back, and was pleased that Elena's little camp was not noticeable at all.

The ride back took longer. For one thing, the ground was slippery now, and for another thing, he did not intend to turn a sweaty horse out when he reached the ranch.

Still, because he had not spent more than an hour and a half in the forest, he was able to reach home in the dark, wet early hours, rub the horse down good before turning it into the corral, and return the poncho to its wooden peg before heading for the bunkhouse.

He undressed outside, tiptoed into the warmth and stygian darkness, slid into bed, and lay there listening to the loudest sound around—his own heartbeats—until sleep came.

Charley was bawling like a bay deer when Young Jim opened his eyes and sat up. Charley had a leak directly over his cot. Cold rainwater had soaked his blankets.

Jeff also sat up, scowling though, at being awakened that way. Charley explained what had happened, then arose swearing and got dressed. Outside, the world was just as dark at five in the morning as it had been at midnight.

Jeff yawned, scratched vigorously, sniffed the air and said, 'No wood-cutting today,' and rolled out reaching for his britches.

Charley had the stove crackling before he groped along the table for the lamp, and lighted it. He then opened the door, sniffed, peered at the fish-belly sky, closed the door and went back for his hat. 'Amos is stirring,' he announced. 'There's a light in the cookshack . . . But as soon as this rain lets up, he'll be hard to live with.'

Jeff was dressing beside his bunk as he glanced over where Young Jim was pulling on his boots. He did not comment on Charley's observation because they all knew how Amos's arthritis acted up when the weather was damp. 'There'll be harness to mend, or wagonwheels to be pulled, or something to do,' he muttered.

Charley looked wry. 'Yeah. There's always something to be done. Shoe the damned saddle-stock, or something. Jeff, what we'd ought to do is head for town and hoist a few. It's been more'n a month, you know.'

Amos beat his triangle and the men hadn't even shaved nor washed yet. Evidently old Amos had arisen well before anyone else.

The older men went out back to wash, but all Young Jim had to do, since he only shaved once in a blue moon, was scrub, comb water through his taffy hair, brush his teeth and clamp the hat atop his head as he struck out for the cookshack—with a beating heart.

Amos looked darkly doorward as Young Jim walked in. George had not appeared yet, either, so evidently Amos had caught all of them unprepared. The *cosinero* bobbed his head and growled. 'Glad to see at least *one* of you fellers got the decency to show up when I ring for breakfast . . . Where's Charley and Jeff—don't tell me; they're out back cleaning up. You know, when I was your age, if a man didn't come runnin' when someone beat the bell for mealtime, he damned well went hungry.'

Young Jim closed the door, savored the good-smelling warmth, and offered to help, but Amos had done it all an hour earlier. He declined the offer, but his grumbly expression smoothed out a little.

'Just set down, boy, and wrap your fangs around this batch of biscuits I made. Fresh as a new day and light as a feather . . . But damned if I know why I go to all the trouble.'

George came in, shiny-faced and wearing his blanket-coat although it was not really chilly out, just damp and clammy. He winked at Young Jim, looked over where

Amos had his back to the room, at the oven, gathered all he had to know from the lines of the cook's back, then sighed and went over to his place at the table, and sat.

'Darned good rain,' he announced, as Amos brought the pan of golden biscuits and set the pan atop a plate so as not to scorch the wood. 'If it keeps it up all day, then quits, we'll have feed into late July.'

Amos snorted. 'If it quits.' He turned back towards the stove as Jeff and Charley stamped off mud outside, then entered and blinked in the lamplight because it was still as dark as the inside of a well, in the yard and out across all the visible countryside.

Charley still had in mind going down to Kremmling, but he did not mention it because George spoke up first about the day's work.

'There's something we been putting off for years,' he told the others. 'Cleaning up the barn. There's junk down there taking up space that I tossed down twenty years ago.'

Charley ate his breakfast stoically, and Jeff glanced sidewards at him a time or two, but Charley would not look up. Hell! it would be miserable riding through the rainfall to town, and back, anyway.

Chapter Eight
A RIDDLE

Charley and Young Jim had seven wagon-wheels to roll from the barn over to the shoeing-shed, which was probably where they should have been stacked in the first place, since the shoeing-shed was also the ranch workshop, as well as the tool-shed. It was where the forge and anvils were; where any work on the wagons around the place was done. But those also happened to be large wheels, and crossing the rain-slippery yard with them, in the downpour, was not the most enjoyable thing Charley could have thought about doing, so he swore a little, then waited over in the shoeing-shed until Young Jim rolled a wheel across, too, and they waited a drying moment before dashing back for the next pair of wheels.

George and Jeff began in the harness-room. There was a pile of broken straps and discarded odds and ends in one corner as high as Jeff's knees, which they began sorting through. Anything with hardware on it, buckles, keepers, steel rings, they kept back. Hardware was not only expensive, it was also hard to come by. Everything else they pitched into a discard-pile, and before they had sorted out more than half the junk, George stood up to roll a smoke, and leaned upon one of the saddles when he said, 'I suppose a man had ought to keep a box in here, instead of throwing everything into the corner. Then, once in a while, he could take the box out and burn it.'

George started to light his cigarette, then paused, looked a little perplexedly at Jeff, and slowly turned, allowing the match to die in his fingers. Jeff stood up. 'What's the matter?'

George dropped the dead match and ran his hand over the saddle he'd been leaning against. He looked up. 'Wet. Feel it for yourself, Jeff.' As Jeff felt the soggy leather, George looked upwards. There was no sign of a leak in the roof. He lowered his head and scowled. 'Look there—mud in the stirrups, Jeff.'

They silently studied the saddle, felt the mud in the stirrups, stood in puzzled silence for a long while, until they could hear Young Jim and Charley grasping the last of the wagon-wheels for the trip across the yard, then Jeff said, 'I don't understand it, George. Unless he rode out last night.'

George slept up at the main-house, so his next remark was valid. 'You were in the bunkhouse. You and Charley.'

Jeff frowned at the soggy saddle. 'He went to bed when we did, and when we woke up this morning, he was right there, George, in his bunk.' Jeff gazed at his employer. 'He could have *snuck* out. After Charley and I went to sleep, he could have snuck out—but why in hell would he do that, and especially last night in a rain-storm?'

George lit the cigarette, blew smoke, then said, 'Come along,' and walked out of the harness-room. Charley and Young Jim were loping through the rain towards the barn. George stood in narrow-eyed silence watching. When they were at the big doorless opening, he said, 'You fellers can drag the harness out to the pole and maybe grease and soap it, if you're of a mind to,' then he turned and walked on down through the barn with Jeff behind him, out into the rainfall and around to the north side of the structure where the corrals were.

He planted a boot upon a low stringer, pulled his hat lower, spat out the cigarette which had sputtered in the rain, and raked the humped-up horses yonder with an eye made wise and shrewd and knowledgeable about horses over a long lifetime in which horses had been more important than almost any other tool of his stockman's trade.

Jeff leaned there, too, looking in, but of all the animals there, head-hung and wet-shiny, no particular horse looked any different from his mates.

George pointed towards a large, powerful bay horse. 'There he is. See under his jaw where a throat-latch was, and behind his left front leg, low down, where the cinch was pulled snug.'

Beneath the horse, too, where rainwater could not reach for the simplest of all reasons: free running water does not run uphill, there was matted hair, also pressed flat by a saddle cinch.

Jeff climbed over to catch the horse and kneel in the rainfall to look beneath him. Then he returned word-lessly to his employer's side of the fence and took up his stance again.

'You're right,' he exclaimed softly. 'He was rode last night.'

They exchanged a look, rain running from the front of curved, wide hatbrims. Jeff said, 'I'll go ask him,' and George shook his head. 'Not yet, Jeff. Tell you what— go on over to the bunkhouse and look around in there. If he had muds on his boots when he came back last night, there should be some on the floor. Make damned certain before you brace a man. Go along.'

Hinman turned alone to the barn and sauntered back in the direction of the harness-room. He paused to watch Young Jim and Charley getting organized to

clean and oil the first set of harness. Charley had a cigarette drooping from his mouth, unlit. That made
Hinman smile. It was the criteria of bad manners in
range country to smoke inside a barn. Charley wouldn't
light up, but he chewed on the end of his cigarette.

Young Jim worked silently and steadily. George
studied him thoughtfully, and when Charley looked up,
George said, 'Sure a shame, the condition a man'll let
his harness get into, isn't it?'

Charley answered ambivalently, since he was strictly
a saddle-man, and only sat behind horses when whatever it was, could not be done astride one of them. 'The
leather's a little dry and dirty, for a fact, but it don't get
used enough to make much difference.'

George looked out into the soggy yard, then back
again. 'If the rain'll let up this afternoon, the ground had
ought to be dry enough tomorrow for us to drive up to
the trees.'

'Yeah,' conceded Charley dryly, 'drive *up,* but it
won't be dry enough for us to drive *back* for maybe a
week. Big logs are heavy.'

George had not been watching for anything from
Young Jim, and had not been expecting anything, but
despite this he noticed the tall youth's shoulders hunch
a little, saw his head drop down, cocked, so he could
hear every word, and also noticed how his busy hands
became briefly unoccupied.

Hinman strolled on, entered the harness-room and
after a solemn look at Young Jim's soggy saddle, went
back to work sorting scrap leather.

By the time Jeff returned the pair of men outside at the

saddle pole greasing and cleaning harness, were on their second set, and were casually talking.

Jeff leaned close to report. 'Mud under his bunk.'

George shook his head irritably. 'What in hell do you suppose he was up to?'

Jeff had no idea. He moved slightly to one side to repile horse-blankets as he replied. 'I don't know, and with this rainfall we aren't going to be able to back-track him.' Jeff worked for a moment, then straightened back. 'Where's the tarp for the chuck-wagon?' he asked. George leaned back in order to see over there.

'Maybe it's deeper down.'

'I looked,' replied Jeff, and dropped to one knee to shuffle through the loose pile of cloth and canvas. 'See for yourself, it's not here.'

Jeff turned baffled eyes upon Hinman. The rancher kept looking at the rumpled pile of canvas. Finally, he said, 'I wonder, Jeff,' and without explaining what he meant, George arose, went over where the ponchos were hanging, and felt through until he found the one he thought might be there, pulled part of it out to show the moisture and the glistening shininess, and let the poncho fall back.

He said nothing until he was over beside the range-boss, and meanwhile, those two voices out yonder came intermittently as Young Jim and Charley pursued what-ever topic they had under discussion.

'If he took a horse, and the tarp, and wore a poncho,' stated Hinman softly, 'then he was setting up a camp. Why else would he take the canvas? . . . Jeff, get over to the cookshack. If he was settin' up a camp, he'd more than likely take food along.'

Jeff left the harness-room heading towards the front of the barn, George went back to sorting leather, indifferently now, though, because his mind was otherwise occupied, and outside Young Jim laughed at something Charley had said. George listened, because Young Jim rarely laughed aloud.

He did not have any idea why Young Jim would be setting up a secret camp. He could imagine no reason for the youth to do anything like that—unless it was in his mind to run off. But that didn't seem reasonable. The lad had plenty of opportunities to leave over the past couple of years. The first year would have been when most kids would have gone. This was his third year on the Hinman place, and he was always right there, eager to learn, proud of his association with the Circle H cow outfit . . . It didn't make sense, but nevertheless there were the damned facts.

Jeff returned and beat water off his hat before entering the harness-room again. Charley, sleeves rolled to his elbows, called over to him. 'Most folks got enough sense to stay in out of the rain.'

Jeff grinned. 'Most folks,' he said, and walked into the harness-room.

George saw the gleam in the rangeboss's eyes, and turned to face him. 'Well?'

'According to Amos there might be some tinned food gone, but he don't keep that close a tally on the shelves. But the bottle of quinine and some other medicines are gone.'

George scowled. 'Medicine?'

'Amos showed me. He was mad as a hornet. I told him not to say a word, and not even to *look* like we know anything.'

'Medicine,' muttered George.

Jeff reshaped his soggy hat and dropped it upon his head. 'We got someone sneaking away with a tarp, George, which will make a decent tent, and we got a feller sneaking away with food and medicine. *And,* if you'll figure back from the time Young Jim got back last evening, you'll come to the conclusion that he was gone most of the day. In fact, *all* of the day, just marking the trees. Now hell, that don't usually take more'n about six hours, including riding up there and riding back. He was up there maybe ten hours . . . Then, last night, he went back up there. I'll bet my pay on it. Where else would he have gone, in the rain, with all that stuff to set up camp with?'

George continued to scowl silently for a moment, then he said, 'Why?'

Jeff shrugged broad shoulders. 'All I can figure out is to set up a camp. Maybe so's when he gets ready he can run off.'

'That don't explain the medicine, Jeff.'

'Well; maybe he figures he might get sick or something, when he's on the trail.'

George disdained this. 'Hell; young bucks aren't like old grannies. Anyway, he's never been sick. Never taken any medicine since he's been here. No; it's more than that.'

Charley appeared in the doorway burdened with the set of cleaned and oiled harness. Jeff moved to hold the door for him. Between them, they got the harness back upon its rack, then Charley reached for the light-harness, the rigging used on the top-buggy and the spring-wagon, vehicles which only required one horse. As he shouldered all that dangling leather he looked over at George, and what George and Jeff had accomplished thus far. He did not look as though he thought they had done as much as they should have, but he said nothing and stamped back outside calling for Young Jim to lend a hand at lining out the light-harness.

A gradual brightness came into the day beyond the barn. No one noticed for a short while, not until the dripping water was audible and a little more warmth replaced most of the clammy chill. Charley looked out, and said, 'It's stopped raining, by golly.' He went ahead to the opening and looked upwards and around. There were definite signs that the clouds were breaking up. Charley was pleased. He did not like being building-bound. He never begrudged a good rainfall, but all the same he was happy when one came—then went.

An hour later, the sun shone through; almost immediately the warming earth gave off a light, vaporous-like miasma, and wood in the barn-roof 'worked', cracked and rubbed, as the process of drying out got under way.

By the time the work was done in the barn, there were only remnants of ragged clouds across an immaculate pale azure sky. The men finished their work and walked up front to take stock, and George quietly said, 'Maybe we could strip down the wagons this afternoon, and head up-country first thing in the morning with axes and saws.'

He had been watching Young Jim when he said this, looking casual and acting that way, too, but his narrowed, shrewd eyes did not miss the slow stiffening which came over the youth.

Amos poked his head from the cookshack and bawled down the yard. 'I got left-over sage hen, with dumplings, if anyone's hungry.'

Chapter Nine
GETTING READY

Amos ate with them, complaining about his rheumatism setting in, and offering to anyone who cared to look, a knotty hand which was exaggeratedly bent into a claw, but only George looked up, the others were so accustomed to this they went right on eating.

George showed an unusual degree of solicitation. 'Rub on your liniment,' he said, 'and after we eat, Young Jim can stay up here and lend you a hand cleaning up, and getting things ready for supper.'

Amos blinked, then immediately brightened. He even went after the coffeepot and refilled all their cups without being asked. Then he became more loquacious than usual, and for a change praised something—the recent rainfall.

Charley eyed old Amos wryly, but said nothing, and when the three older men had departed, walking through the drying mud in the direction of the bunkhouse, with George leading, Charley offered an opinion.

'You're lettin' it happen too often, George. You'll

spoil that old cranky bastard. He'll be expectin' the lad to he'p him every couple of days.'

George said nothing. He walked into the bunkhouse, flung his hat upon the table and pointed to a bench. Charley sat down, slowly acquiring a baffled expression as the other two men, still silent and stony-faced, eased down upon the opposite bench.

'What the hell's wrong?' enquired Charley.

They told him, beginning with the wet saddle and going right on up to the missing medicine.

Charley sat there like a man who had just been struck without any reason. He looked from Jeff to George. He flattened his mouth and puckered up his eyes. He probably would have been able to come up with some defensive argument, if they hadn't burdened him with the entire story. And also if either one of them had attributed what Young Jim had done to something underhanded or dishonest, but all they could say about Young Jim's *reason,* was that they didn't know what it could be— unless he was just preparing things for an eventual, swift running-off, and Charley stamped on that the moment it was said.

'How? On foot? He wouldn't take one of our horses—that'd be stealing, and the boy's no thief, you can take it from me, he's no thief. I'd have known it by now if he was. There's one thing I can't abide, a damned thief, and a *horse*thief . . . there's nothing worse. No sir, the boy wouldn't do that.'

Jeff quietly said, 'All right, Charley. Then he figures to walk. Just how does a feller pack all that stuff on his back? That old tarp weighs at least sixty-five pounds.'

Charley arose and went to plant his legs wide with his back to the cold stove. There hadn't been any heat in the thing since morning, but a man's winter-long habits are buried deep. He looked at George and Jeff from a face twisted with concern and bafflement.

'Maybe old Amos misplaced that quinine and stuff,' he muttered.

George's answer was quietly offered. 'And the canvas, Charley? And the soaking-wet saddle? Quit trying to make excuses for the lad. Hell, we're not accusing him of anything. Not yet anyway. We're just trying to figure out why in hell he done it. There's no reason; he's liked here; he knows damned well we *want* him here. It's kind of like having—well—maybe having a kid-brother around, or a nephew—or something. He's a decent lad. You said yourself he'd make one of the best hands we've had on the place, in a year or two . . . What hits me hardest, is that I can't figure for the life of me why he'd want to leave us.'

Charley swore. 'Gawddamn it anyway. All the time we've spent with him—and all. Well; there's just one way, and that's to get him down here right now and ask him just what in the hell he thinks he's doing.'

'Nope,' exclaimed George. 'That's not how we're going to work it.'

'How then?' demanded Charley.

'Maybe he'll go back tonight.'

Charley and Jeff stared at their employer. One of them said, 'Trail him?'

George nodded. 'Trail him.'

'That's plumb underhanded,' growled Charley.

George did not argue this point. 'Maybe. But there's something about what he's done, and the way he did it, that I can't figure out, exactly.' He looked up. 'You know what I suspect? There's someone else out there; maybe some sick feller, which would be why he took the medicine.'

'Well why didn't he just come right out and tell us?' asked Charley. 'Hell's bells, we're not a bunch of—'

'And if it's an outlaw?' asked George.

Charley blinked and turned silent.

'It's sure as hell someone he don't want us to know about,' stated George. '*If* I'm right, but it could just be like we figured at first, that he's setting out a camp for running off. Anyway, if he goes back tonight, we're going along too—a mile back. You fellers watch, tonight. Pretend you're sleeping and keep a close watch.'

Jeff agreed with this, and Charley eventually returned to the table to drop down and listen as the other two men worked out the details for a close surveillance of Young Jim. The entire matter though, as George emphasized, had to be handled very circumspectly. They could not allow Young Jim to have any idea he was being watched.

They eventually went back outside, in the humid afternoon heat, trooped across to the shoeing-shed where there was always something to be done, and talked, argued, and theorized away half the afternoon, until Young Jim came along to smilingly inform them that he now had the cleanest hands on the ranch, from all that dishwater.

Jeff detached himself from the working crew and ambled off in the direction of the cookshack. Amos was smoking a foul little pipe on the porch and raised squinty, doubting eyes as the rangeboss climbed the two wide steps and leaned upon an upright post.

'How'd you make out?' Jim asked, and old Amos immediately took umbrage.

'What you fellers worrying about? That I couldn't bring it off like nothing had happened, and like I didn't know nothing?'

'Well, did you bring it off, Amos?'

'Of course,' snarled the old man, who removed his pipe and looked steadily upwards. 'Are you plumb certain, Jeff? Hell, that's as nice a lad as I've known in many a year. Considerate, he is, and—well—some gentle and kindly. The rest of it just done set up with what he is.'

Jeff had to agree. 'Yeah, I know, Amos. But—the medicine is gone isn't it? And there's the other things. But I think what's getting George down, is that Young Jim didn't confide in him. You know how George looks on the lad . . . having no sons of his own, and all.'

Amos leaned to knock dottle from the evil little pipe and drop the thing into a torn shirt-pocket. 'Gawd damn,' he sighed. 'I've lived so damned long, Jeff, and just when I get some idea there's hope in the next generation . . . Well; what you fellers figure to do?'

'Watch him day and night. Keep him in someone's sight all the time. The next time he sneaks away, we're going to trail him.'

'And what'll you do when you find his camp?'

75

Jeff was not sure about this. 'That'll be up to George.'

Amos slowly inclined his head in agreement with Jeff's revelation. 'You know what I'd do, if I was in George's boots? When I confronted him, up there, I'd give him the horse he's riding, and send him on his way without another word.' Amos arose to return to his kitchen. 'Hell of a note,' he said, reaching for the door. 'Just when you're plumb certain about someone—something like this.' He walked inside and let the door rattle closed.

Jeff rolled a smoke, lit it, stood a while upon the shaded porch, then headed back in the direction of the shoeing-shed.

The yard was drying fast, and that resurrected sun was making up for the wasted morning by adding unnecessary heat to the sogginess, with the result that there was such high humidity it sapped men and animals.

Young Jim wilted along towards late afternoon, and Charley, who knew exactly how tough and untiring the youth ordinarily was, took this wilting as fresh evidence that Young Jim had not got as much sleep last night as he had needed. But he said nothing, as he and Young Jim got wheel-jacks beneath one of the big wagons in order to pull wheels and slather grease on axles.

Jeff and George were behind the barn working on the other wagon. There was nothing easy about stripping down a heavy rig, and the weather did not make it any easier, either. Young Jim met Jeff at the water-trough, and smiled at him as they both dunked their heads after drinking. 'Hot,' he said.

Jeff agreed. 'Yeah. Drains all the energy right out of a

man. How you fellers making out?'

'We got the sideboards off and most of the planking. Won't be long before we'll have it finished.'

'Then maybe you two could hone-up the axes and look to the set in the saws.'

Young Jim nodded and turned back across the yard. When he told Charley what they were to do as soon as they finished stripping the wagon to its running gear, Charley was agreeable. At least their next job would be inside the shed, where there was blessed, cool shade.

He pointed to a pole balanced across a large flat rock. 'Bear down on that while I jockey this blasted wheel back on.' Charley was strong, age notwithstanding. As soon as the bed tilted enough, he grasped two wrist-sized spokes, lifted the wheel and eased it ahead, dead-centre onto the tapered axle. Then he spun on the nut with the reversed thread, hauled it up snug, and nodded for Young Jim to let the rig back down, gently. As he was reaching for the wrench to tighten the nut, Charley said, 'If we was to light out of here before sunup in the morning, we could likely get the wagons loaded, and be on our way back by mid-afternoon. What do you think?'

Young Jim's frank reply dragged a little. 'I expect we could. The trees are all on flat ground. We can drop them, then drive the rigs right up and lever them aboard—except that they're big trees, Charley, and they'll be awful heavy. The wagons'll likely stick.'

Charley thought this was probably true. 'Well, in that case maybe we'd better take along a tarp and some food, and camp up there; drop the trees tomorrow. Take our time about limbing them and all, then maybe load them on the next day. By then, if this sun keeps up hot like it is now, the ground'll be plenty hard by day after tomorrow.' He leaned upon the big wheel watching Young Jim. 'What do you think about that idea?'

Young Jim did not give his opinion. 'It'll be up to George,' he mumbled, and went back where the tail-gate had been to begin loosening the bolts for the final dismantling of superfluous fittings.

Charley drew forth his limp bandana and rubbed surplus grease and dirt off his hands as he watched Young Jim. Eventually, he also went to the rear of the rig and went to work, but now he was silent for so long that Young Jim finally asked if he didn't want to go inside the shed and start working on their hand-tools, leaving Young Jim to finish up outside.

Charley removed his hat, dragged a grimy sleeve across his red face, and glanced over in the direction of the barn. 'All right,' he replied. 'You can help inside, when you're finished here, then we'd better go snake out the teamhorses and go over them, too. All it'll take to make me melt plumb away this afternoon would be to discover that one of them danged beasts has cast a shoe. Today sure as hell ain't a day for real hard work.'

There was a huge grinding-wheel in the shed which a man sat behind and worked the bicycle-like pedals on a pair of steel arms fastened to the centre of the wheel. The harder the man pumped, the faster the grinding-wheel turned.

By the time Young Jim came inside, his shirt sticking to him, Charley had all the tools placed atop a workbench. Young Jim straddled the wooden seat and began pumping the wheel. Charley stood in front holding an axe. They ground six axes, then set up three cross-cuts in two wooden vices, and Charley showed Young Jim how to get the precise angle, or 'set', to each tooth. He grinned once, saying, 'Young Jim, if you'd known there was work like to running a cow outfit, would you still want to be a cowboy?'

Young Jim smiled back. 'Yeah. I would have, Charley. But I guess mostly because—well—the cowboys I've met out here, they're sure nice folks.'

Charley stared, and turned slowly back to the work in front of him, his expression showing more bewilderment than ever.

Chapter Ten
'DAMN IT ALL'

George made his decision, then left it up to Jeff to tell the others, while he ambled off in the direction of the main-house.

Jeff was out back at the wash-rack scrubbing before supper and looked over his shoulder when Charley, trailed by Young Jim, came around there to lean in the pleasant shade.

Jeff told them: 'We're going to harness up before breakfast, then eat, fetch along some food, our bedrolls, the tools and a canvas, and roll out of here ahead of sunup.'

Charley looked at Young Jim. 'See,' he crowed. 'My idea, exactly.'

Young Jim said nothing. Neither did Jeff as he flung away the basinful of water so the next man could step up.

A mangy old dog-coyote went loping on a southwesterly angle no more than two hundred yards out, and when Jeff saw him and grunted, straightening up to stare, the coyote stopped, raised his head, turned his sharp face in the direction of the men, and stared.

Charley, with soap and water on his cheeks, peered from puckered eyes. 'And not a gun within reach,' he said.

The coyote hadn't shed yet. There was matted winter hair still clinging in patches, but especially along his undersides. Charley said, 'Worms. They all got 'em,' and turned back to the basin.

Young Jim watched the dog-coyote until the thin, sinewy animal started loping away, then he turned. 'How do you know he's wormy, Charley?'

Jeff had to answer because Charley had soap over his entire face. 'The long hair on his belly. It's the same with horses and cattle. That's how you tell when critters need worming.'

Young Jim, who knew these men and their way of teasing him without cracking a smile, looked doubtful. But he said nothing.

They finished cleaning up and went inside the bunkhouse to rest a little before Amos beat the triangle for supper. Charley pitched his soiled clothing atop the bunk. He had to walk over to the pump this evening and do some laundry.

Outside, a man's high halloo rang softly in the waning

day, coming from a considerable distance. Charley and Jeff exchanged a look, then headed for the door.

The rider was coming slowly, on a big gray horse who had his head down, swinging, as he walked right along. The rider had a floppy straw hat atop a bald head. He was a large, fleshy man, who had at one time, been a very formidable specimen, but that had been perhaps thirty years earlier.

His name was Clifford Blackman. He owned Blackman's Bar down in Kremmling, and although the men in front of the bunkhouse knew him well enough, they were surprised to find him this far from his saloon so late in the day—or for that matter, at any other time of the day. Cliff Blackman was not ordinarily a horseback-rider.

George walked out upon the veranda of the main-house and leaned to watch the saloon-owner ride on in, down by the barn, and get heavily to the ground.

George started down to greet his visitor. The men from the bunkhouse were already heading that way.

Blackman draped his floppy hat from the saddlehorn, pulled an enormous blue bandana from a coat pocket and pulled it across his perspiring bald head, twice. Then he shook his head as the Circle H men strode up.

'A man's got a right to figure, when it's drizzling rain, that it won't be hot out.' He boomed. 'And that just goes to prove a man can't even trust Mother Nature. By gawd, it's got to be a hunnert and fifty degrees out there—and sticky. I must have sweat off ten pounds.'

Charley grinned. 'Your horse ought to like that Cliff. What you doing up here, anyway? You can't make it back to town before the saloon's full this evening. That ought to pain you—not being there to hear all them silver coins go jingling into your cash-drawer.'

The big man looked down his nose at Charley. 'How come you to allow your damned hired hands to insult folks, George, when they come visiting?'

Hinman smiled. 'I'll tell you the key to Charley Wagner. If he insults you, he likes you. If he don't open his mouth around you, he don't like you. What *were* you doing up here, Cliff?'

The big, fleshy man flung out both arms as though to cut a wide swath through the rangeriders. 'Let me at the trough,' he boomed, and headed for the stone watering place. The men turned to watch, amused. Young Jim unlooped the horse's reins and led him around the rack over in the same direction. Over there, he loosened the cincha and slipped off the animal's bridle. When Blackman was finished, and turned away dripping wet, blowing like a whale, Young Jim led the horse on up. The animal was very thirsty.

Blackman walked back, somewhat refreshed, and said, 'Some fellers went up from town this morning to see if there really was In'ians in the hills. I went along, until the drizzle stopped and that blasted heat come, then I turned back. I don't know what I went along for anyway, except that exercise don't hurt a man. Looking at mangy redskins isn't any novelty. I've seen whole nations of 'em in my time.'

George slowly scowled. 'They didn't come by here, Cliff.'

Blackman treated that indifferently. 'No need,

George. They just wanted to poke around in the hills a little. No need to bother you about permission to do something like that.'

George's look of annoyance deepened. 'It happens, Cliff, I don't take kindly to that sort of thing.'

The big fleshy man stopped and stared. 'You don't? Since when? You never say anything about folks going up there with wagons for winter wood, nor for fellers from town going into the mountains after elk, late in the year.'

'This is different,' explained Hinman. 'If there are In'ians up there, I don't want them stirred up by a bunch of gun-happy townsmen. You get them mad, and whose place is closest, and whose livestock is handiest? Not yours, Cliff; not the homes or animals of any of the fellers in Kremmling.'

Big Clifford Blackman drew out his limp blue bandana and dried his face and neck slowly and thoughtfully, then he said, 'Hell, they won't find any In'ians. I've yet to go out with a posse of townsmen who didn't make enough noise in a stalk to wake the dead. And it's gawd-awful hot, the closer a man rides towards those slopes. They'll do like I did; they'll turn back. Anyway, they don't have any food with 'em.' This seemed to lead Blackman to a fresh train of thought. He broadly smiled at George Hinman. 'They'll be coming along in an hour or so, starving, and you'll have to feed 'em to get 'em on towards home.' Blackman chuckled.

Young Jim, standing at the trough beside the horse, was staring from a pale face at the saloonman. None of his range-riding companions were looking in his direc-

83

tion. They were concentrating on Blackman and Hinman. Young Jim said, 'I'll stall your horse,' to Blackman, and led the animal over into the cool, dark barn.

Charley turned and peered from beneath his tilted-down droopy hatbrim in the direction from which the saloon-owner had ridden. The land was shimmery and empty as far, and a whole lot farther, than he could see. 'If they're coming,' he opined, 'they'd better hurry up, because Amos sure gets mad when he has to feed two shifts.'

Blackman ignored that, and studied George Hinman, whose irritation was apparent. 'George,' he said, placatingly, 'if there's In'ians up there, I'll eat my hat. There hasn't been anyone report seeing smoke above the tree-tops. Let the darned idiots have their fun—they'll ride their rears raw, make up some big lies to tell their kids, and everyone else, and that'll be the end of it. Hell, if there *was* In'ians up there, by now we'd have heard about it down in town. The army'd be riding in, plus some In'ian Agents, and a whole flock of those other buzzards who hang out around reservations.'

Amos came out upon the cookshack porch and peered down through the gathering shadows to make a head-count. He already knew, from having heard Blackman's shout from half a mile out, there would be another set of boots planted under his supper table this evening. He just wanted to make sure it was only one man. He did not really object to feeding visitors. In fact, because they had some kind of news to impart, he liked having strangers ride in.

84

Having made his count, Amos went back inside to make the necessary preparations to feed another man.

George got over being annoyed, which was characteristic of him, but he still did not relent in his sentiments. 'I'm going to put up some signs,' he said, as the four men turned over in the direction of the bunkhouse porch to sit in the shade. 'It's not that I object very much about folks going into the mountains, it's just that I figure they'd ought to have enough manners to come by the ranch first, and find out if it's all right.'

Blackman wisely did not press his view of this sort of restriction. Like most men who had grown up in a land where free-roaming was traditional, he did not like to hear this kind of talk, but on the other hand George Hinman would not be a good man to arouse into anger.

They pulled up chairs and eased down. There was still soggy heat in the day, but as the sun sank lower its direct rays were unable to find the cooler places, so the weather began to become noticeably more pleasant.

Blackman hooked big feet and massive legs over the porch railing and tilted back his chair. He emitted a great sigh. 'I'm too damned old for this tomfoolishness,' he admitted. 'But you know—every now and then a man forgets what he *is,* remembers what he *was,* and does something silly like I done—riding out with those young bucks like that.'

He looked dolorously dead ahead, over where the wagon Young Jim and Charley had stripped down, was standing, and beyond the wagon, out across the grasslands to the point where visibility was limited by the coming of evening.

'Some dancing girls come to town last week,' he said, indifferently, in the nature of a man passing along news to people who seldom got any news.

Jeff looked over. 'Pretty ones, Cliff?'

Blackman considered his answer before offering it. He was, like George Hinman, far enough along in years to be both interested in dancing girls, at the same time he was critical of them.

'Well, one of 'em was a big blonde. She was pretty. No more'n maybe thirty, big and stout with a nice smile. But the other ladies was a mite longer in the tooth. Anyway, the Lady's Altar Society got after the marshal to run them out of town.'

Jeff scowled. 'He did that.'

Blackman sighed again, settling all his vast bulk more comfortably into the burdened chair. 'Yeah. But you got to understand something, Jeff. His wife is president of the Altar Society this year. Now—that may not mean much to a feller who's never been married, but let me tell you something: Womenfolk can make it almighty uncomfortable around a house if they're of a mind to. Take my word for it, Jeff. I been married, one way or another, six times. Believe me, just when you been thinkin' all day how things is going to be right after supper—hell.' Blackman spat out that last word with such a loud sound of monumental disgust and pain, that George Hinman laughed.

Charley started to roll a smoke, then raised his head slightly and cocked it. A moment later he flung down the half-rolled cigarette and sprang up to run in the direction of the barn.

George and Jeff looked as nonplussed by this unique behavior as did the saloonman.

Charley raced into the barn, ran mid-way down, then halted. The place was empty. He swung back, wrenched open the harness-room door, saw that the saddle was missing, and let go with a shouted curse.

The men on the bunkhouse porch heard that. George suddenly sprang to his feet, intuition telling them all he had to know. 'Come along,' he snapped at Jeff. 'Cliff; tell Amos I said to feed you.'

Blackman made no attempt to get out of his chair, but he looked after the running rangemen with his mouth hanging open.

Charley was already heading for the corral to snake out a horse when George and Jeff came in, up front. Charley gestured with his rope-hand. 'He's gone. His saddle and bridle are gone.'

George and Jeff did not wait, they also headed swiftly for the harness-room. Jeff finally said, 'Damn it all.' That was all he said, and George did not even say that much as they hurried to also catch mounts and saddle up.

Chapter Eleven
DANGER

They scattered to get their guns, and wasted another few minutes after doing that, buckling Winchester boots to their saddles.

Charley eyed the darkening sky as they rode from the yard with Cliff Blackman still watching from the bunkhouse porch. 'Not enough light to track him by,' Charley mumbled, but this was not entirely accurate. It would have been, though, if there hadn't been recent rainfall. They could make out the dug-in gouges where a running horse had hit hard before springing ahead to hit hard again and again.

They did not really need the tracks. As they loped steadily up-country towards the distant forest, George, whose calm and discerning judgment had not failed him up to this point, only made one mistake—well—actually *two* mistakes. He said, 'He's sure as hell hiding some feller up there. Otherwise he wouldn't have run off like that, knowing we'd be curious. He was desperate. I think maybe he's sure-enough got a wounded outlaw up there.'

George was wrong because it was not an outlaw Young Jim was racing towards, and it was not even a male critter. But otherwise he was right; Young Jim *had* been agitated by what Cliff Blackman had reported, and he *was* riding full tilt through the night towards his hidden friend.

Charley said, 'An In'ian, George? Cliff was talking about those townsmen riding up there looking for In'ians.'

George scoffed at that. 'Wouldn't be an In'ian. They hide from us. Anyway, the other In'ians would take care of some feller if he got hurt.'

Charley could have argued about this, but he did not really care whether it was an Indian or not, and he was also inclined to believe the last part of what George had said. Indians took care of their own.

The most important thing, right at this moment, was to find Young Jim and see just what, exactly, was happening.

The night was warm and still, but as time passed a faint chill arrived. It was not cold enough for any of them to untie the jackets behind their cantles, but it would be that cold before they got back home again.

The sky was clear, with pale stars turning more brilliant as the darkness deepened. There was no moon, but even if there had been, a new moon would not have added to the light. Nor did they particularly require good visibility, for although they eventually lost sight of the horse-tracks they had been following, by the time this had happened they knew exactly where they were going. Providing Young Jim did not change course, and he did not vary a yard in his haste to reach the Crow girl. Charley would have, and so would George Hinman. They would have zigzagged, ridden through the rocks, and done a number of other small things to confuse pursuers and hide their sign, but even if Young Jim had known how to do those things, he probably would not have taken the time.

George and Charley discussed this, deducing from it that the youth was worried. They then followed out this train of thought and arrived at the conclusion that if Young Jim was fearful those townsmen would find his secret place and its occupant, since the townsmen would not go into the real, back-country, mountains, and since Young Jim would not have done this, either, when he had blazed the trees so that wagons could pull in beside them, why then, the fugitive had to be close to the forest's lower edge, perhaps no more than a few hundred yards up through the trees.

Jeff listened to the talk saying nothing, but apparently accepting what the other two men said, because when George dropped his horse to a quick walk, and gestured for Charley to lope ahead and quarter until he picked up the tracks again, Jeff pointed ahead towards the dim, jumbled darkness where tree-ranks stood.

'There's a little run-off creek to the west about a half mile.'

George said, 'I know,' in a disinterested tone. He was watching Charley moving like a wraith back and forth in a widening sweep. Charley was bending from his saddle as he rode.

Jeff rolled a smoke, lit it behind his hat, and gazed up where the fragrant and fresh-washed forest firmed up into a solid dark wall dead ahead of them. He sighed and shook his head. Unless they were almighty lucky, that darned kid was going to get them all into trouble. It was not very clever of them to be riding up into the forest, no matter what the reason, and especially at night. But with a bunch of townsmen maybe up in there, armed and spooked, plus some raggedy-pantsed Indians who would also be spooked if they heard horsemen coming, or saw them . . .

'Over here,' Charley sang out in a muted call, sitting his saddle and gesturing.

They loped over, saw the sign towards which Charley was pointing, then stopped dead still for the first time since leaving the ranch, gazing up where the forbidding darkness of the trees did not look very friendly nor inviting.

Charley said, 'Looks like the tracks run along beside that little creek, straight up through the trees.' He paused, then also said, 'George, we better leave our horses tied and do this on foot. A man don't make any noise walking over pine-needles, but a horse sure does.'

They dismounted to lead their animals the last few yards, and were tying them when Jeff turned towards the others with a screwed up face. 'You fellers smell smoke?'

George and Charley sniffed, then replied that they did not smell anything. There was a faint little breeze coming low to the ground, down from the higher back-country. Evidently it had shifted as Jeff was asking his question, because moments later Jeff did not smell anything, either.

They pulled out the saddleguns, then stood a little uncertainly facing the deeper forest, none of them happy about being there, and at least one of them—Charley—annoyed at the person who had got them up there.

George said, 'Jeff, stay to my left. Charley, stay to my right, and no matter what else you do, don't lose sight of me. We got to sweep through here quiet as mice, and keep each other in sight.'

'Suppose,' muttered Jeff, 'it's a band of In'ians.'

Charley replied to that. 'Then you'd better remember all your prayers—but most important, don't point your gun at one unless he's pointing his gun at you. Folks can usually *talk* their way out of bad situations a heap better

91

than they can *shoot* their way out.'

They moved ahead, deeper into the trees, but warily and slowly. When Jeff, who was on George's left side closer to the little brawling creek, picked up the horse-sign again in the punky earth next to the creek, they had the satisfaction of knowing that they were at least on the right trail.

Jeff asked an unanswerable question as he straightened back from studying the imprints, and peered ahead. 'How damned far did he go, up in here?'

Charley raised a hand and lightly touched Hinman's arm. 'Smell,' he grunted, and set an example by raising his head and turning it a little from side to side. '*Now* I smell smoke,' he said.

George made his judgment, too. 'But it's a long ways off, Charley.'

That made them all feel relieved. It also confirmed something for them; there *were* people up in the hills. Whether they were Indians or those damned townsmen from Kremmling, posed a fresh question, but the main one had been settled. There *were* people up ahead, somewhere.

Charley grounded his carbine to lean on it. 'We should have brought Cliff along,' he muttered. 'At least he's big enough to hide behind.'

George gestured for Charley to move away a short distance. They then started their wary advance again.

That little ground-swell-breeze dwindled down to nothing. It never entirely died away, but it was scarcely noticeable, and overhead interlocking tree-tops blocked out all but an occasional ragged little patch of starshine.

The forest was utterly silent. When one of them made even the smallest sound as they moved cautiously onward, it carried to the ears of them all.

Charley and his employer had done this sort of thing before, but under somewhat different circumstances. They had been members of a larger armed party. It did nothing for their sense of well-being to reflect that if the Indians were up ahead of them somewhere, they were going to be hopelessly outnumbered.

Neither did it do much for their sense of survival, being in the forest at night. But in another way, for the two older men, George Hinman and Charley Wagner, it was a little like rolling back the years. Neither one of them had time to reflect upon men of their ages being in this kind of a situation. They acted, and reacted, as each of them had, thirty years earlier. For a while they were young men again.

George, who was less spontaneous than Charley, less liable to speak out quickly, concentrated fully upon the onward course they were following, and it was this intense attention that finally caused him to raise an arm, then beckon his companions in closer.

He pointed earthward with the barrel of his Winchester. 'Been a horse tied to that tree.' The others leaned to make certain. 'He was tied there for quite a spell.'

Jeff said, 'Maybe it was Young Jim's horse, last night,' and Charley looked disgustedly at him. 'It rained,' he exclaimed scornfully. 'Young Jim wasn't up here more'n an hour or such a matter, and the rain would have washed out his sign. That there sign still shows, despite the rain, because the tied horse stood there maybe all day long.'

The rebuked rangeboss turned to look elsewhere. Visibility was very limited. In fact, none of them could see more than a yard or two in any direction.

Jeff thought he saw scuffed earth and needles over beside the creek and looked harder before drawing the attention of his companions to that vaguely disturbed area. Finally, he moved ahead and to his left a little. At the same time someone up ahead, and more to the right, suddenly said, 'They're here. By gawd I seen the tethered horse no more'n thirty minutes ago.'

Charley and George sank to one knee and turned to stone. Jeff stopped dead still too. That disgruntled voice had not belonged to an Indian.

George finally whispered. 'The men from town sure as hell.'

That same annoyed voice floated back down through the trees again. 'I *know* they're here.' A second man mumbled unintelligibly, and the first man replied curtly, 'Yeah? Well, when you get a pouch of money for helping the army find the bastards, you'll feel different.'

Charley spat, leaned on his carbine and stared steadily up where those men were moving through. Jeff eased back beside George and also sank to one knee. 'We better call to them,' he whispered.

A sudden thunderous gunshot erupted. It caught the Circle H men completely off-guard. They dropped flat in the darkness, pressing hard into the damp pine-needles.

Up ahead a man squawked, and a deafening reply of

ragged gunfire broke out.

Jeff lifted his head. Initially, he had thought those men up ahead were shooting back down at him, and his companions, but wherever the first shot had been sent, it was easy to discern that the volley which followed after was being fired northward, not southward.

Jeff was no less puzzled than were Charley and George. If there had been a moment when the rangemen could have called ahead, identifying themselves to the townsmen, it had come and gone. Now, to sing out behind those men would be to invite a fusillade.

Up ahead, that same thunderous weapon roared a second time. Again, the less deafening but very loud carbines and Colts in the hands of the town posse, blazed away, and this time it was possible for the rangemen to see an occasional muzzleflash.

George leaned towards Charley. 'That first shot—and the other one a minute ago, came from a horse pistol.'

Charley bobbed his head. 'They got 'em an In'ian cornered sure as hell. No one else still uses those old cannons.'

The question became a matter of whether to try and intercede, or whether to just lie there quietly and be spectators. Anything they did now which would let the excited possemen up ahead know there were other armed men behind them, could not be done without risk.

Jeff made the older men smile. He pulled a little off the ground and spoke through the diminishing gunfire. 'Right this minute I'd trade jobs with old Amos, and throw in a new hat to clinch the trade.'

The horse-pistol cut loose again, and immediately afterwards the townsmen responded with additional gunfire, but it became clear now to the watchers, that the townsmen were spreading out, were expanding their toehold until it cut someone off on three sides, east, west, and southward. They were apparently trying to stealthily surround their pinned-down enemy with the horse pistol.

Charley said, 'They got him. They got the poor son of a bitch sure as I'm lying here.'

Chapter Twelve
A NEAR THING

Into the lull which followed the last response to the single shot of the horse pistol, a man with an angry voice called out.

'Gawddamn you, there ain't a chance in the world of you gettin' away. Quit shooting and give up, or we're coming in after you!'

It was not a reassuring ultimatum. Charley shook his head over it. 'They don't want him to give up.'

So much time passed that it seemed improbable that there would be an answer. But it came, and when the first words sounded, the men on the ground far back were stunned.

'You come in after us and you're going to wish you hadn't. Why don't you just leave us alone. We haven't done anything.'

George said, 'That's Young Jim!'

Jeff and Charley raised up slightly, but it was Charley

who took the initiative. He let go with a ringing call to the townsmen up ahead.

'You sons of bitches get the hell out of here! You got no business up in here!'

Someone, probably a fearful or agitated individual, turned at the sound of Charley's voice, and cut loose with a hand-gun. Charley had been hoping this might happen. He raised his carbine, aimed low in the direction of the muzzleflash, and fired. Then he levered up again, swung the gun slightly, and fired again. He did this three times, ground-sluicing his blind shots.

A bawling voice through the darkness called on the men up there to swing around, to face this new enemy. George Hinman swore with feeling when the first fusillade erupted, and rolled frantically for the protection of a large tree. Jeff rolled too, but Charley did not move until he had fired his Winchester empty, pinning down their adversaries. Charley was a fierce man, when conditions demanded it. Single-handedly, he scattered the townsmen. Between his gunshots they could be heard crashing left and right through the forest trying to get clear.

When Charley fired his gun empty, he turned disdainfully and walked to a tree, where he leaned, his back to the enemy reloading. Charley was fired up to kill someone.

George took advantage of the hush to call ahead.

'This is George Hinman. You fellers listen to me. You're trespassing, and you don't know what the hell you're doing stirring up those In'ians. If the whole bunch of 'em comes down here, we're all of us going to get trampled. Go on back to your horses, while you still can, and head back to Kremmling. If you don't, you're going to have more fightin' on your hands than you can handle. Us on one side, the In'ians on the other side. You hear me?'

For a while there was no answer, then a raspy voice said, 'Hinman, we got some In'ians cornered. They're worth something to the army. They're off the reservation and—.'

'You silly bastard,' exclaimed Charley in monumental disgust. 'That wasn't no In'ians just answered you. That was one of our riders. In'ians my tailbone! Now you do what Mister Hinman said—or you're going to get hurt.'

Again, there was a prolonged silence before the man with the raspy voice spoke again. 'Mister Hinman; this here is Kale Roberts, from the liverybarn in town. I'll come down and talk with you.'

George said, 'All right,' and looked over where Charley was standing, reloaded Winchester in both hands. Charley was watching for someone to appear, and George, who knew Charley very well, shook his head at the cowboy. 'Let him come,' he said quietly.

Charley groaned, but when a lanky, sinewy man appeared, clutching a Colt at his side, Charley did nothing.

Kale Roberts was a thin, tall man. He was known around Kremmling as a man who drank hard, periodically, but he did not have a reputation as a troublemaker.

George Hinman stepped around to face the townsman, Winchester held in the crook of one arm. Robert gestured backwards with his free hand as he walked on up. 'There's In'ians back there, Mister Hinman. We seen their sign all over up in here.'

George was flinty. 'In the dark?'

'No; we been scoutin' for 'em all afternoon. We seen the sign before it got dark. In fact, they had a little camp right yonder when one of our fellers first come onto 'em, and by the time the rest of us got over here, they'd moved it back a few hundred yards. Another one come up, some time between afternoon and evenin' then they moved their—.'

'Wait a minute,' exclaimed George. 'This other feller who came up—he was on horseback?'

'Yeah.'

George said, 'That wasn't an In'ian, Kale. That man works for me . . . Now damn it all, I'm going to tell you something. You got no business up in here. You—.'

'We're trying to help the army, Mister Hinman.'

'Did the army ask you to help it?' demanded George.

'No, but they don't even know where these redskins are, and we can save 'em a lot of riding just by bringing in some of the—.'

Charley, fuming and silent up until now, interrupted. 'Kale, for Chris'zake, there's a whole *band* of In'ians up here, if there's any at all. You town-cowboys are just lucky you didn't try that silly surround on the whole bunch. You aren't going to bring any redskins in, and you'll be damned lucky if you get back to Kremmling alive. All that shootin' is bound to have stirred up everyone for five miles.'

Charley stood and glared. So did Jeff, but he had nothing to say, until the liverybarn-hostler tried once

99

more to explain his motivation. 'We figure they're worth maybe two dollars a head to the army, or the federal marshal, or maybe their In'ian Agent.'

'You got an awful thick skull,' said Jeff. 'George and Charley just told you—that gunfire's got the whole band fired-up by now. We *all* got to get out of here, and do it fast.'

George gestured with his pistol. 'Go on back to your friends, Kale. Charley and Jeff and I'll follow along. Well; what are you waiting for?'

The hostler turned reluctantly and shuffled back the way he had come. They did not any of them have very far to walk. Men appeared like wraiths from among the trees. There looked to be about twelve or fourteen of them. Mostly, they were chagrined at having fired on the Circle H men, but there were two men whose resentment lingered, and one of these said, 'Why'n hell didn't you fellers sing out? We thought you was more In'ians.'

'Sure,' growled George, 'and get shot at by a bunch of trigger-happy townsmen.' He looked around, recognizing most of the men. 'Wherever you left your horses—go on back there, get aboard and head for town. The fun's over.'

A man said, 'We're losing money,' and sounded sullenly disgruntled about this.

'Better'n losing your damned life,' spat Charley Wagner, and turned away, to shoulder through the little band heading northward through the trees. When he had covered a dozen yards he called out.

'Hey, Young Jim—where are you?'

The answer came so close by that Charley jumped

when Young Jim softly said, 'Here, Charley,' and stepped from the shadows holding that big old horse pistol.

Charley glared, then looked down at the pistol. 'Where in hell did you get that damned blunderbuss? Son, don't you know the man behind one of those things is in more danger than anyone out front of it? Those are relics; they ain't shootable.'

Young Jim grinned. 'This one is, Charley.'

The older man raised hard eyes. 'Who you got hidden out up in here? Go along, now, and don't argue. Show me.' Charley motioned peremptorily with his Winchester. 'Walk along, now.'

Young Jim obediently turned, passing back and forth through the huge old trees leaving Charley to stamp along behind him. When he got to the hidden small camp where he'd barely had time to re-string the old canvas before the townsmen attacked, Charley stopped dead still.

The Crow girl was sitting there, where a little pale starshine found its way down through high tree-tops. She looked up at Charley without showing expression, and without saying a word.

He leaned to poke aside some pine-needles, saw the moss and one of the dishtowels torn into strips. He also saw the quinine bottle and the other medicine, then he shoved back his hat and looked squarely at the girl. 'You hurt?' he asked.

She nodded, but it was Young Jim who spoke out. 'She was shot in the leg, Charley, when they were making a run for it back to these mountains, where they used to make meat each autumn.'

Charley digested this in silence. 'Where did you get hit?' he asked, and Elena rolled back the blanket to let him see the swollen, purplish upper leg with its draining holes. Charley sank to one knee for a closer look, then he pursed his lips and glanced up at Young Jim.

'You found her up here, yesterday?'

Young Jim nodded. 'Yeah. By accident. Charley; how did you and George and Jeff know I was up here, tonight?'

'That,' exclaimed Charley Wagner, 'can wait. Anyway, as a skulker, you're not worth much. You left sign all over the place.' He got back to his feet as George and Jeff came striding up. In brief sentences Charley explained about the gunshot Indian girl. George shook his head. Without looking at Young Jim, he said, 'Boy; what do you think we are? Did you figure we'd shoot her, or something? Any time a man's got real problems—well hell—that's what a man's got friends for.'

Charley glanced over his shoulder where the sounds of men slogging eastward through the lower-down forest were audible. He looked enquiringly, and Jeff Pelton said, 'They left—the damned fools.'

The girl spoke to George Hinman. 'It was up to me. He wanted to help me reach a doctor. I told him not to tell anyone. Not even you.'

George gazed steadily at the wound. 'Lady, I know you figure you can take care of that thing, and you likely can, but it'll take a long time, and meanwhile you're sitting here unable to walk, and when those townsmen get back to Kremmling, they're going to tell the constable down there—and maybe the army, too, if it's arrived by now—and they'll be coming back up here to find you, and there you'll be, like a sitting duck.'

He turned slightly to face Young Jim. 'The next time someone tells you not to do something, and you know a damned sight better—don't you listen to 'em. You do what *you* know had ought to be done. You understand me?'

Young Jim understood perfectly. 'Yes sir.'

'Now you and Jeff go on back to the ranch, hitch the team, fill the spring wagon with straw, and get on back up here. And don't kill the horses. No one's going to come around from town until long after you've got back.' George turned towards his rangeboss. 'The big sorrels, Jeff.'

Young Jim was reluctant to leave, but with three sets of irate eyes upon him, he finally acquiesced. Elena watched him depart from an impassive face.

Charley turned to hunting for dry twigs because the night was turning more chilly by the hour. George leaned aside his Winchester, sat down near the girl, and wordlessly rolled and lit a smoke. Then he gazed at her.

Her eyes widened when he spoke in Absarokan, telling her in slowly spoken words of his wife, how they had met one late autumn while he had been hunting in the mountains, telling her of their life together, and of how she died and was now buried in her special place on the ranch. Then he swung back to English to say, 'Young Jim did the right thing, to help you, but it would have been better if he had let the rest of us know.'

George smiled at the lovely girl. 'You see, we figured he was hiding a renegade or an outlaw.'

She did not smile back. 'I am a renegade. I am a Crow off the reservation.'

Charley came up and went to work skuffing clear the drying needles, kicking away everything that would burn, then making his little fire upon the wet earth beneath. As he worked he grumbled something about food, and Elena handed him her *parfleche,* which Charley took, then hunkered there examining the pouch wryly. It had been many years . . . He smiled and handed it back, without saying a word.

The heat, coming in under the old stretched canvas from the open front of the shelter, rapidly changed the chilly interior. George asked the girl if she were feverish. Her reply was that she was not today, although the two previous days she had been feverish, off and on.

He asked about the leg, and she told them that although her entire body had been sore and hot for a few days, now there was no particular pain unless she moved the wounded leg. Then her white teeth showed. 'I am heavy. Young Jim could hardly carry me when we moved up to this new place . . . The leg hurt when we did that.'

George and Charley, captivated by the lovely smile, continued to sit and regard the girl without speaking for a while. Young Jim had no doubt been motivated by his humanitarian instincts. They were sure of that. But this Crow girl was beautiful, and they were also sure this had something to do with it, too.

Chapter Thirteen
THE WAIT

The girl had rested and slept, off and on, all day long, but the pair of older men had not only missed their sleep, but had also been deprived of supper. They finally agreed to eat a little of the food Young Jim had brought, and while they were doing that, the Crow girl looked past into the pitchblende night southward of the canvas shelter, out beyond where the meager little flicking flames could reach, and said, 'It is now all right.'

Charley felt hair coming up along the nape of his neck. He and George looked first at the girl, saw that she was looking at something behind them, and turned very slowly.

There were three buck-Indians, large men, all with the typical braids of Crows, standing motionless just beyond the firelight. They were heavily armed.

The girl spoke curtly in her native tongue, then gestured towards the pair of older men sitting inside the shelter with her, and one of the big bucks walked soundlessly ahead, grounded his carbine and squatted down. He was not a full-blood, he was far too fair for that, but because he wore Crow braids and his attire was typically Crow, until he squatted down where firelight shone against his broad, round face, neither George nor Charley were aware that he was not a full-blood.

Charley, eyeing the shadowy forms farther out, asked how many Indians were close by. The big buck answered curtly. 'Fifty, sixty. Why, you want to fight us?'

The girl snapped a guttural sentence, and the big buck looked briefly at her, then back at Charley and George. He seemed little affected by what she had said.

George, deciding they were not in the best position either of them had ever been in, offered friendship by saying, 'We ran off some townsmen who came up here.'

'Yeah,' said the big buck. 'Indian-hunting. We knew they were here. And we stayed away because they would go back after dark. Then all the shooting started up.' The Indian looked at Elena. 'Did you hit one?'

Elena gazed stonily at the buck for a long time before answering him. 'No. I did not hit one. I did not shoot at one. Young Jim used my father's pistol. He shot at them. He is the man who found me, and brought me medicine, this canvas, and plenty of food.'

The Indian's broad brow furrowed. 'Young Jim?'

George said, 'He works for me. He's one of my Circle H rangeriders.'

The Indian's brow cleared. 'White man, then.'

George and Charley said nothing, but they both watched the big Indian. He was not their friend, but as yet he had made no move to disarm them. Actually, if he had as many strong-hearts out through the forest as he had said—fifty or sixty of them—the two white men did not have to be disarmed. They were prisoners of the Crows, weapons or no weapons.

Elena did not yield an inch to the buck. 'Young Jim helped me.'

This made no impression on the big 'breed Indian.

106

'You could have stayed here with the band. Now— hell—they know we are here.'

'They knew anyway,' Elena threw at him, scornfully. 'Young Jim knew. So did these men.'

The buck looked at Charley. The old rangerider did not speak, he simply shrugged wide shoulders and picked up some twigs to feed their dying small fire.

It was George who took up the discussion. 'It don't matter now whether we knew or not. Those townsmen we ran off will head back to the settlement and tell everyone they can find that there's In'ians up in here.'

The buck stared into the fire for a while, silent and motionless. Then he finally said, 'We will take her back with us.'

George stared. 'How, on your shoulders?' He pointed to the covered, wounded leg. 'She's got a bad hurt. You jostle her around and that thing'll start bleeding, and maybe you'll make it back up there with her—but she'll be bled out. No. You leave her here. I sent back for a wagon. We'll take her to the ranch, let her take all the time she needs to get well, then it'll be up to her.'

The buck fixed George with a stony, tawny stare. 'We will take her back with us.'

Elena spoke quietly. 'You listen. This man's wife was one of us. Her brother was Red Horse. This man told me. You know Red Horse. I will go with them in the wagon.'

The buck dropped his gaze back to the little fire for a moment, then he turned and called quietly in his native tongue. Four strong-hearts glided out of the forest-night, and Charley used this distraction to slide his right hand into the dark shadows on the right side of his body.

He drew the Colt and cocked it. No one moved for a moment, or uttered a sound. The four standing Indians stared steadily at the tilted gunbarrel, so close it could not miss. He said, 'The girl is hurt. She wants to go back with us in a wagon which will be along directly, so's she can get good care. Gents; that's what she wants, and that's what she's going to get . . . We just run off a band of whiteskins, and if we got to, we'll do the same with you. But we're not here to fight, only to help the girl. It's up to you.'

A very dark Indian with his braids encased in weasel-skin, spoke gutturally to the 'breed-Indian, and got a sharp rough retort. George, who understood, said, 'She's *not* a girl, she is a *woman*. She *can* make the decision.'

The very dark Indian gazed at George, then spoke again to the 'breed-Indian, but this time in reservation-English. 'She can go with 'em. It's only a woman. We heard what this man said about gawddamn men from the settlement going back to find friends and bring 'em back. We got to go back now. Quick. Strike camp and go away before the army comes.'

Charley silently holstered his sixgun, then turned a speculative gaze upon the big 'breed. 'He's right, bronco. You're wasting time here. Those men, when they get down to Kremmling, will tell everyone. They will maybe telegraph to the army.'

George took it up. In quiet Absarokan, he said, 'I understand how you think. But you cannot fight the army. Not any more. Listen to me, now. This is my land.

No one can cross it unless I say they can. But the army will cross it anyway. I can stop the townsmen, though. I can turn them back, and unless the army had already come here, to the settlement, I will turn back the others. That will give you a day, maybe two or three days . . . Well?'

The four standing Crows listened, then turned their attention upon the big 'breed-Indian, and when he did not speak, that very dark man with the weasel-skin braids, spoke again.

'We will go back.' The dark Indian jutted his jaw towards the silent 'breed. 'He can stay with you, or he can go back with us. He is not our leader, he is only her brother.'

The white men were surprised. There had been nothing in the exchange between the girl and the buck-Indian to indicate a relationship. They hadn't even addressed each another as kinsmen, nor had either of them shown any noticeable fondness for the other.

Without another word, the four strong-hearts turned away. Charley fished out his tobacco sack and leaned forward as he painstakingly rolled a smoke, which he lit using a twig from the fire. Then, having evidently decided that the 'breed-Indian had had enough time to make his decision, Charley said, 'If you go back with us, bronco, you better get that chip off your shoulder.'

The buck's tawny eyes came up slowly, fiercely. 'I wouldn't walk ten feet in your tracks,' he stated. Then turned on his sister. 'These men have talked you into going with them!'

Elena's retort was short. 'You know that is not true.

No man has ever talked me into doing anything. Not even you!'

The buck slowly unwound up to his full height in the tent-opening, blocking out nearly all the rearward darkness. He was a powerful man. Charley and George kept a wary eye on him. Indians could be very unpredictable.

Then he turned on his heel and stalked out into the dark forest, and within moments was out of sight among the trees.

Charley placed a palm upon the ground to push upright, but the girl stopped him. 'He will not shoot you from out there. He has gone.' She looked past, into the darkness, and seemed unhappy, so George spoke to her. 'You can go back when you're able to ride again. Don't worry. I'll give you a good horse and we'll go back with you. Meanwhile, there is a doctor over the mountains, and we'll send for him.'

The girl's answer was dogged. 'I don't want a doctor. I need clean water and time. That is all.'

It was probably all she would need, at that. About the only thing a doctor could do, she would be unable to do for herself, would be to trim away the ragged flesh, suture the wound so that when it healed, finally, the scar would be less objectionable, but, since the wound was between her knee and thigh it would not be visible anyway; whether they got the doctor or not, she would heal.

George understood her. 'You'll get what you want. If you don't want the doctor, you don't have to see him.' He smiled at her. 'I'd like to have you at the ranch.'

The girl's tawny eyes lingered on George.

Somewhere, in the distance, an owl called. Even more distantly it was answered by another owl. Elena looked at the blanket as she said, 'My brother. The others answered so that he can find them.'

For the first time, she seemed sad.

Charley ducked out to search for more dry wood to keep their small fire burning. It was late, now, and the night was turning increasingly chilly.

George smoked, gazed into the embers, and sat for a long while without moving or speaking. It had been many years since he'd sat like this, with a beautiful Crow girl, and the pain of recollection was like a dull knife.

Charley returned, dumped his armload of faggots, got comfortable and yawned behind an upraised hand. Elena told him to sleep, but he made no effort to do that, instead he smiled at her as he said, 'Old bones, young lady. That's all that's wrong with me, I got old bones.' When she smiled understandingly back, he then said, 'Where is your father?'

'Dead. He died three years ago on the reservation. Pneumonia.'

'And your mother?'

'I never knew her. I was born under a big log in the dead of winter when my people were being hunted. She froze to death before my father could find us.'

Charley's gaze drifted back to the fire. 'Hell of a note,' he said, which was an understatement, which would have been an understatement coming from anyone but Charley Wagner, who was not gifted enough to say something more truly appropriate, but the *feeling* was there, in him, and in fact, men like Charley and George more truly understood and appreciated what the girl had said, than younger men could have, because they had *seen* things like that.

Then he said, 'Maybe there's a place,' and the girl's eyes studied old Charley's face before she replied, a trifle shyly.

'Yes, there is a place. But which place is it—the Crow place like the Sand Hills—or is it the white man's place, Heaven, which I learned about in the mission school?'

Charley said something that made George stare at him. 'What the hell's the difference?' He gestured. 'It's all alike—these mountains or the next mountains. These pine trees, or other pine trees a thousand miles from here. This creek, or some other creek. The Sand Hills, Heaven, whatever you want to call it, it's all the same.' He looked steadily at Elena. 'Just—no enemies, there. No warparties. Plenty of free horses and good hunting. Plenty of little children and good women. Plenty of time, and no aches in the bones.'

Elena's gaze at Charley was stone-steady. 'I like your place best,' she told him, gravely. 'I'm glad I found you. What is your name?'

'Charley Wagner. This here is George Hinman. He's the owner. We work for him.' Charley, who had never been praised very much had no defense against it, tried to change the subject by saying, 'George, those two fellers ought to be on their way back, by now.'

George agreed. Then he also said, 'And maybe so are those idiots from Kremmling.'

112

A little, sluggish cold breeze came to make their fire flicker, and to work its way inside their shelter, then it lifted off the ground on its southward way and made the tree-tops whisper a little. Otherwise, all the people inside the improvised shelter had to do was wait. They were all accustomed to doing this, nor did it seem to bother them that they said very little while they waited. They were not from an environment which made people feel that silence was awkward and should be broken by a lot of talk.

From time to time, Charley pitched twigs on their fire. It got warmer inside the shelter, and when George turned to say something, Charley was sitting there, cross-legged, slumped, somehow managing to balance himself in an upright position while he slept.

Chapter Fourteen
TO CIRCLE H

It was not quite dawn when the wagon came into the foothills, but by the time the men got Elena made comfortable, got everything loaded and were ready to head back, dawn was breaking.

Charley and George rode up front, on either side of the wagon talking to Jeff, telling him about the Indians who had arrived during his absence, but Young Jim rode near the tail-gate. He and the lovely Crow girl talked a little. She told him of the Indians, and of her brother, and she also told him what Charley Wagner had told her about that Other Place. She seemed to have been very impressed by this.

Young Jim wasn't; he never thought of death or dying. At his age, it would have been odd if he had thought about them.

The sun came, finally, soaring over the hard, dark crust of the easterly world like an immense lemon, about the same color and the same stippled texture. In another few hours it would be flooding the world with heat. It was going to be a hot, muggy day, and as the men passed slowly southward, they instinctively speculated on how close to home they would be, before the full weight of heat arrived.

The ground was still soft. That rainfall had revitalized all growing things. There were wildflowers among the grass-stalks, and new, pale leaves on the few oaks they passed.

Young Jim was solicitous, but Elena smiled her assurance. Maybe Young Jim did not suspect it, but the older men knew exactly what she was doing. The bumping and bouncing *did* hurt her, but it was not right to show someone you were in pain when they had done so much to help you.

The only thing that was said, up near the front of the wagon, was Charley's quiet observation that if that had been anyone else, in the wagon back yonder, they'd be groaning, and if it had been old Amos, he'd be turning the air blue every time Jeff neglected to straddle a hole.

They were within sight of the log buildings when George suggested that Charley lope ahead and tell Amos. Charley started out, covered about three hundred yards, then turned back. The watching men were surprised.

Charley pointed out with a rigid right arm while he was still some little distance away. There was a bunched-up party of horsemen swinging inland from over the hazy east, heading directly for the little wagon-caravan from Circle H.

'Trouble,' muttered Jeff, and raised his lines to slap the rumps of the team. He looked over his shoulder. 'Girl; I hate to do this, but we got to make it to the yard.' He slapped, the team, started out their plodding reverie, hit the collars and jerked the wagon forward.

Young Jim and Charley rode up on either side of George, then loped along behind the wagon, also heading for the yard.

They made it handily. Those oncoming horsemen did not seem anxious to rush ahead, but neither did they alter course. It was this inexorable slowness that both-ered George. He dismounted out front of the barn, and said, 'Young Jim, you and Charley carry her to the mainhouse. Tell Amos to settle her in the back bed-room—then you fellers stay up there.'

Jeff, eyeing the riders, decided he had enough time, so he led the horses inside and flung off their harness, then corralled them. He was just strolling back out front towards the tie-rack, where George Hinman was leaning, hat pulled low to shield his eyes from the sun-light, as the riders came into the yard.

The foremost man had a star on his shirt-front. They all knew him. His name was John Taylor. He was a tough, often disagreeable man, who had once been imprisoned for shooting a Mexican in the back in Kremmling. The others were about equally divided between rangemen and townsmen. Of the townsmen, several were recognizable as having been with that band up in the foothills last night.

The riders were not looking at George or Jeff, they were staring up in the direction of the main-house where Charley and Young Jim had just disappeared inside with their burden.

Constable Taylor reined down, clasped both hands atop his saddlehorn and gazed squintily at George Hinman. 'Folks are raising hell,' he said, gruffly. 'They don't like it, you fellers firing on those boys from town, last night.'

George's reply to that was matter-of-fact. 'John; we didn't *half* fire on 'em, until they started it. Anyway, no one was hurt.'

'Yeah, but you run them off, George.'

'That's my right. I own that land and I don't like trespassers. Especially a bunch of nitwits with guns.'

'There's In'ians up in there,' stated Constable Taylor.

George did not deny it. 'All right, John, then there's redskins up there—but that's not your business. It's up to the reservation authorities and the army. And me. I live closest to those hills, and it'll be my livestock gets shot up, if some idiots go redskin-hunting up there and stir those people up and get 'em mad. And John—I did those boys a favor. If they'd still been around when the broncos came along to see what all the gunfire was about—you'd have likely had a wagonload of corpses.'

One of the other horsemen scoffed. 'What broncos?' he demanded. 'We could have handled 'em.'

Jeff looked at this man. 'Fifty or sixty of 'em?' he asked quietly.

Constable Taylor scowled. 'How many?'

'The ones who came down where we was sitting with the wounded girl, said there was fifty or sixty strong-hearts,' replied Jeff. 'John, that's one hell of a mess of mad Indians.'

Constable Taylor agreed. 'Yes it is.' He looked in the direction of the house again. 'You brought one of 'em back, George?'

'A girl with a bad bullet-wound in the leg.'

'Who shot her? Not one of the lads from—?'

'She got shot reaching the mountains down here when she was running with the rest of her band. No one around here did it, John, but it's a bad wound and it'll take months for it to mend. We brought her down to the ranch to get decent care.'

John Taylor frowned at his horse's ears. Eventually he said, 'Fifty strong-hearts—that means there's got to be maybe a hundred, maybe a hundred and fifty Crows back in the mountains, all told. That's a big party of Indians.'

George's answer was blunt. 'Keep folks in town and out of my hills, John. The army's probably already heading this way. But until it shows up, I don't want any more men riding up there.'

It probably was nothing George Hinman had said which moved the hard-eyed lawman to nod his agreement, it was probably the thought of half a hundred stirred-up, fully armed Crow bronco-bucks. 'Let the army handle it,' he assented, and lifted his rein-hand.

'Can the girl talk to folks, George?'

Hinman lied. 'She's too sick, John. Give her a few days, then she can.'

Taylor accepted that. 'All right. I'll telegraph the army when we get back to town. They'll likely want to talk to her, too.'

The possemen did not offer a single objection when Constable Taylor led the way on across the yard, south-easterly, back in the direction of town. No doubt the size of the fighting contingent accompanying those break-out-Crows had made a deep impression upon them, too.

Jeff removed his hat, wiped off sweat and dropped the hat back atop his head as he leaned on the tie-rack watching the possemen leaving the yard. 'I'm gettin' gray,' he complained. 'Just since last night.'

Amos came forth upon the cookshack porch holding his heavy old buffalo-rifle and craning around to also watch the possemen. George shook his head. 'If he'd fired that blasted thing it would have broken his shoulder, stampeded every horse for five miles, and deafened all the rest of us.'

They ambled over to the main-house.

Young Jim met them at the front door with a broad smile, and a Winchester in his sweaty hands. Amos came through from out back, still dragging his big-bored old buffalo gun. He stood straighter than he had in months, and there was a fierce look to his flashing eyes.

'Good thing,' he crowed. 'Good thing them high-binders didn't offer us no trouble.'

George, looking skeptically at the old rifle, gravely

nodded. Then he said, 'We got a patient, Amos. She'll need some hot broth and some fresh bandaging, and—.'

'Don't tell me what hurt folks need, damn it all,' exploded old Amos, and turned indignantly back in the direction of his kitchen, hauling the old rifle along with him.

Jeff sighed. 'Well; we're sure as hell home again,' he mumbled, as George tossed aside his hat and followed Young Jim towards the distant hallway door. Just as they got over there, George said, 'Young Jim—the carbine. Put it back in the rack. No sense going to see her with a gun in your hands.'

While Young Jim headed for the wall-rack, George and Jeff walked down the hall in the direction of Charley's gruff voice.

Elena was sitting in the middle of the large bed, still clutching her *parfleche* bag and her blanket. Charley was scolding her, but gently. 'You don't need the pouch, and we'll fetch you a cleaner blanket. Young Jim and I'll bring in some hot water directly, and a tub, then you can get settled in. Girl, you got nothing to fear around here. Everyone around is your friend—but with Amos, you got to handle him just right.'

George entered the room, straddled a chair and told her about the possemen from Kremmling, and what the constable had said about calling for the army. But he made it sound almost a casual thing. 'Your people will be gone a long while before any soldiers reach here.' He then said, 'Elena, they ought to go back. I know—no one likes living on a reservation. But the choice isn't hard to make—fight, or go back. If they fight, they're going to lose.'

She answered tersely. 'They know. I told my brother it was useless; a few old people wanted to go back and make meat one more time. I told him it would make trouble for the people.' She looked steadily at George. 'They will go back, now. Do you know why? Because there is no other place for them to go. Even with a big start on the soldiers—where can they go that they won't find more rangemen or more townsmen, or more soldiers?'

George said, 'Nowhere,' and stood up. 'Young Jim can stay with you for a spell.' He turned and jerked his head at Charley. The three older men trooped back through the house and out to the cookshack. They were ravenous. It did not help, either, that Amos was already boiling the beef to make broth. He looked at them as they straggled into his kitchen, and felt compassionate enough to say, 'Just set at the table. No need to wash-up. You can do that afterwards. I'll rassle you up some decent hot food.'

Charley leaned, dumped his hat down upon the bench, and said, 'It won't be no warmed over sage hen, will it, Amos?'

That was a mistake. The *cosinero* turned on Charley Wagner like a striking rattler. 'Doggone you anyway, Charley. I never yet seen you walk out of here without leaving your plate shiny as new money, and you know confounded well I never fed *any* of you fellers anything that wasn't fitten to eat!'

Charley hung his head. 'You're right,' he muttered.

'Amos, you're plumb right. You're as good a camp-cook as I ever run across.' Charley lifted his head a little at a time, until his tough eyes were fixed fully upon the cook, then he also said, 'If you hadn't been such a fine camp-cook, you old bastard, I'd have shot you long ago.'

Amos glared, searching for something appropriate to say. When he found it, he let Charley have it, hard. 'You, of all folks, bringing an In'ian to the ranch. You—who got no use at all for In'ians. Charley, you're going soft in the head.'

This time, with Charley's color visibly mounting, George broke in with a growl. 'That's enough from the pair of you. Amos, for gosh sakes, we're about half starved.' George turned towards Charley. 'She's not the same breed. She is Crow. The In'ians you got cause to hate was Sioux.'

Charley's eyes widened a fraction. 'What do you know about it?'

'Two years back, in town, I got to talking to a feller from northern Montana. He told he'd heard an old friend of his was working the ranges around Kremmling. Charley Wagner. He told me about his old friend staking a claim and moving in, with his woman, ten, twelve years back.'

Charley kept staring at George. 'What else did he tell you?'

'All of it, Charley. Bloody-hand raiding party came along, left you for dead—and left her plumb dead.'

Amos and Jeff were motionless. George twisted on the bench. 'Amos, fetch that bottle of old popskull you use for snake-bite medicine.'

121

Amos brought the bottle, and the glasses, and did not say a word.

Chapter Fifteen
THE VISITORS

Amos gave them all beef broth the next morning, and when George looked quizzically at him about this, Amos recounted the values of beef broth as told him by his grandmother, who recalled giving it to the wounded on both sides back during the Rebellion, in New England.

Nothing was said, because along with the broth, Amos gave them their customary morning spuds and breakfast steak, but when they got outside Jeff gave it as his opinion that while he had never thought about it before, it was now his opinion that Amos would have done better if he'd followed the nursing profession, rather than the cow profession.

Jeff could have been right, at that. When Young Jim returned to the house, later in the morning, to see how Elena was getting along, he found a vase of flowers on the dresser, the curtains pulled back so she could see out, and some smashed cloves in a dish, which gave off a pungent spicy aroma.

She smiled at him, freshly scrubbed and wearing someone's nightshirt, visible above the blankets. Amos had taken her other clothes to wash them. She said he was like a mother grouse with chicks.

She also said she did not feel right, lying here like this, in a perfectly strange house without another woman around. She had assumed that George Hinman would have re-married.

Young Jim's answer was light. 'If there are no other women around, you got no competition. You'll get *all* the attention.'

She looked steadily at him after he said that, then swung to look out the window where golden sunshine was strengthening the soft, morning brilliance. 'I would like it better if I could walk,' she told him. 'I could work.'

He leaned in the doorway, hat in hand, watching her. She looked more golden that usual, in the reflected, clean sunlight, lying against the white pillow and sheets.

'You're pretty,' he said.

Elena turned towards him. She said nothing, but the way she looked at him made him redden.

'Well,' he explained—lamely. 'I didn't notice it up in the forest. I reckon it was too dark, or something.'

Amos came bustling in with milk toast, shouldered past Young Jim, and winked at him as he said, 'Got to build her up, son. We got to get meat on them bones. Got to keep her healthy and strong so's the healin' will get done quicker.'

Elena raised up, black hair falling down her back. She looked a little pained, or embarrassed, or resigned, it was impossible to tell which it was, when Amos handed her the steaming bowl and the spoon which went with it. She had eaten breakfast not an hour and a half earlier.

'Eat,' exclaimed Amos, gesturing. 'Girl, you got to build up your strength.'

She gazed at the thick, weighty contents of the bowl,

then smiled feebly at Amos and obeyed his order. Young Jim got the feeling she was forcing it down, which she was.

Amos turned, winked again at Young Jim, then went back through the house in the direction of his cook-shack. Elena looked over at Young Jim. 'I'll be so fat I won't be able to run, by the time I can walk,' she complained.

He grinned. 'I think you're good for Amos,' he said. 'I never thought about it before, but Amos needs someone to worry over.' His smile faded but his gaze remained thoughtfully upon her. 'In fact, I think you're good for *all* of us.'

He left, returning to the yard where Charley and Jeff were sorting saddlestock in the corrals, one man cutting, the other man operating the gate. George was on the outside, occasionally calling an instruction, by the time Young Jim got out there.

They had several fourteen-hundred-pound animals which were too big to saddle, so George had decided they would break them to harness. They would, he explained to Young Jim, hitch one of the green horses beside one of the harness-broke horses, when they went up to make wood. It would be a chancy drive up, but the drive back, with logs on the wagons—all the weight any two horses could handle at a walk—the green animals could learn quickly to accommodate the driver.

When the big horses were cut back and closed into a separate corral, Charley and Jeff climbed over the stringers and turned to join Young Jim and George, watching as the big horses nervously eyed the men, and trotted around, heads up, looking for a way to rejoin the other horses.

Young Jim turned to gaze around the yard, where the morning heat was beginning to build. The spindly smoke rising from the cookshack stove-pipe was dwindling. Someone had properly parked the spring-wagon, after it had been left out front of the barn. That would have been Jeff, who was usually very orderly. So much so, at times, that Charley accused him of being like an old granny.

A thin lift of vaporous dun dust was rising down in the far southeast. Young Jim watched it for a while, then spoke quietly to George, beside him.

'Riders coming from the direction of town.'

The big harness-horse-prospects were instantly forgotten. Maybe Young Jim should have got a clue as to why they were all still killing time at unimportant chores around the yard, this morning, instead of riding out as they usually did, by the way his companions turned towards that distant stand of dun dust. All three of the older men showed resolute, tough faces, then Charley broke the silence by saying, 'Expect I'd best go along to the bunkhouse for a moment,' and strolled away.

A moment later Jeff also headed for the bunkhouse, but without speaking, and finally George said, 'Son, go on over to the house, tell Amos to give you my gunbelt, and tell him to never mind that damned old buffler cannon, and lay hold of one of the shotguns in the parlor wall-rack. Hurry along.'

Young Jim hurried.

The horsemen were visible by the time Charley and Jeff returned to the tie-rack out front of the barn, where George was indolently leaning, slitted eyes watching the visitors. They were both wearing guns.

Young Jim came back from the direction of the cook-shack, carrying a holstered Colt dangling from a shell-belt. He wordlessly handed the weapon and belt to George, who, just as wordlessly, buckled it around his middle. Then he said, 'Son, you'd do well to go set with Elena.'

Young Jim shook his head. 'I'll stay here.'

George and Charley turned to look, and the youth did not flinch from their stares. He had never had much occasion to stand up to either of them before. Now, he thought he *did* have such an occasion, and it was clear from his expression that glaring at him was not going to change anything.

George turned back to join Jeff in watching the oncoming riders, but Charley still faced Young Jim. He said, 'All right, then. But you go on over to the bunkhouse, take that old Winchester of mine, and stay right over there, in the doorway, with it in your hands.'

Young Jim looked as pale as he'd looked the day they pulled that calf. He finally moved off, and Charley's speculative eyes followed him. 'Don't use it,' called Charley. 'Just stand there lookin' like you might use it.'

'It's Taylor and a soldier, and some other fellers,' stated George.

'Well, it's too damned early for Santa Claus,' said Charley caustically, and reached to tip down his hat-brim.

The riders dropped to a walk just beyond the yard, and rode past the cookshack heading in the direction of the men at the barn. Suddenly, they all turned to stare at the cookshack doorway. The men down by the barn could not see Amos but they knew he was over there, in the doorway, with a scattergun in his hands, looking fierce.

The riders stopped talking among themselves as they came on. On their left, before they reached the barn-front, they also saw another Hinman-man standing in a doorway holding a gun. Constable Taylor's tough, dissolute features reddened, his wound of a mouth pulled back flat. The soldier at his side, a stocky, whiskered, hawk-nosed man burnt coppery from years of exposure, proceeded to remove his gauntlets as he rode the last fifty yards, glaring at the slouching rangemen by the tie-rack.

The riders strung out behind the soldier and John Taylor, closed up a little, bunched themselves; a man did not have to know much about trouble, to realize that having two men behind him, one with a shotgun, the other a rifle, was bad medicine.

Taylor reined up, lowered his reins and looked stonily at George Hinman. 'This ain't a friendly welcome,' he said.

George's answer was equally as brusque. 'Depends on what you came here for, John.'

'Your wounded Indian,' replied the constable, and gestured. 'This here is Captain Potter. He come along in advance of the cavalry company to scout things up.'

George gravely nodded. 'Glad to know you, Captain . . . The girl don't leave here.'

Potter studied George and the two men leaning there with him. Then he raised his eyes to gaze around the yard, and finally he twisted a little to look over in the direction of the bunkhouse. Young Jim was there, staring back, holding the saddlegun.

Captain Potter hauled up straight in the saddle, facing George. 'I wouldn't defy the law if I were you, Mister Hinman. Your wounded Indian will get good care.'

Charley said, 'She's too sick to be moved.'

Captain Potter's answer to that was predictable. 'Then we'll bring out the company ambulance, when it arrives in Kremmling. It should be along directly; the men made camp on the far side of Rabbit-Ear Pass last night. They'll come up very shortly now.'

George did not take his eyes off the captain. 'She stays. It's her decision, either way.'

'No,' drawled the captain. 'She's a ward of the U.S. government, Mister Hinman.'

Jeff sneered. 'What does that mean? She isn't able to make a decision of her own?'

Captain Potter's eyes flashed. 'If you want to take up the matter of rights and such like, do it with the Adjutant General. I'm only a cavalry officer. I've got my orders.'

Jeff did not relent. 'Your orders don't extend to Hinman-range, Captain.' Jeff jutted his chin in George Hinman's direction. 'He owns this country; it's his orders folks obey.'

Constable Taylor exploded. 'For Chris'zake, George, what's the matter with you? This here feller represents the *army*. You can't buck the United States *Army!*'

George faintly and bitterly smiled. 'I'll bet you I can sure give it one hell of a try, John.'

The constable's mouth fell open. Behind him, the riders who had come along with him from town, also looked nonplussed. Only Captain Potter, who had met cowmen before, was not phased.

'There are sixty troops in the company, Mister Hinman, and a mountain howitzer. Now for gawd's sake be sensible. I guarantee you the wounded squaw'll receive the best medical care anyone can give her, and she'll be safe with us, and in due time she'll be returned to the reservation. Now what can you do that's any better, will you tell me?'

'Yeah,' stated George. 'I can do the same for her, and one more thing you *can't* do; when she's able to walk, I'll give her a horse, some money, some food, and turn her loose. She can go anywhere she wants and become whatever she wants. She can even go back to the reservation, if she's a mind to, but it'll be her decision, Captain, not mine—and sure as hell not the army's.'

Captain Potter began to slowly pull his gauntlets back on as he sat up there staring stonily at George Hinman. Constable Taylor's expression of outrage was tempered by his knowledge that two men with guns were behind him. He finally said, 'George, this here is the stupidest damned thing you ever done. You heard what he said— sixty soldiers and a mountain howitzer. What in gawd's name can you and Jeff and Charley—and the kid yonder—do against *them* odds?'

'Get a lot of publicity, I guess,' replied George, dryly.

'George, let her go!'

'She stays, John!'

Captain Potter lifted his reins. 'Come along, Constable. I know his kind. He'll come around when the column gets up here.' Potter scowled blackly. 'Mister Hinman, I wouldn't try to get her away from here into hiding, if I were you. Let's go back, Constable.'

No one spoke as the riders turned back across the yard riding at a slow walk back in the direction from which they had come, but when they were well beyond the buildings, and two horsemen suddenly split off, one loping westerly the other easterly, Charley said, 'I knew it! I knew they'd do it! Those damned blue-bellied officers is always sly as snakes. Now we got a spy on each side of us.'

'And,' mused Jeff Pelton, 'a little army with a cannon on its way.' He straightened up off the tie-rack. 'I always wanted a pair of gloves like that captain had.'

Amos appeared, without his shotgun, and bellowed across the yard. 'Come eat!'

It was high noon, and none of them had noticed it, except Amos.

Chapter Sixteen
'WE GOT TO OUT-FOX THEM'

For Young Jim the confrontation had been traumatic. He did not eat much, and afterwards while the older men were noisily—and profanely—discussing what might happen, Young Jim went through the house to Elena's bedroom.

She already knew; Amos had told her gleefully how

George Hinman had handled the constable and the army officer, but when Young Jim appeared, she looked distraught rather than pleased or defiant.

'That is all people think about,' she said bitterly to him. 'If it isn't the Indians fighting the settlers and cowmen, they are—both sides—fighting each other. Young Jim—why?'

He had no answer, nor did he feel much better about all this than she felt, but he pretended to, for her sake. 'You don't want to go back, do you? Well, that's all George said—that you had the right to make up your own mind, the army didn't have the right to do it for you.'

She looked bleak. 'Young Jim—Mister Hinman came along forty years too late.'

He did not understand her meaning. 'Maybe. But I can tell you one thing: He's not going to back down. I've worked for him going onto three years. He don't back down when he's right.'

Her tawny eyes widened with incredulity. '. . . Fight the army, just the five of you?'

Young Jim did not answer because, as he stood considering the way she said that, and the way she was staring at him, it *didn't* sound very sane. 'You're worth it,' he told her, and smiled.

She held out a hand to him. He walked over and took it, held it not knowing what else to do with it, hot flushes running up through him. Then she said something that made him forget her soft, warm hand lying in his hand.

'If you rode north, and went fast, Young Jim, you

could find my people, and if you could explain to my brother that the soldiers are trying to take me away by force, and the Circle H men are trying to help me, I think he would bring the strong-hearts.'

Young Jim let go of her hand. 'I'll tell George,' he said, and hurried from the room.

But the men in the cookshack were unreceptive. As Amos said, dragging in a band of fighting Crows who were already in trouble for an unauthorized departure from the reservation, would only make it worse all around—even if the Indians could come, which he doubted very much, since almost no Indian thought whites fighting whites was such a bad idea.

George strolled through the house to talk with Elena, and meanwhile, Charley Wagner smoked two cigarettes, then strolled to the yard to see if those two spies were still squatting out there. They were. Charley called them some unflattering names, and when George suddenly appeared on the front veranda, calling him, Charley left off his name-calling and walked over.

'Go to town,' said George, 'and hand this note to the preacher. And Charley—be careful. Don't let John see you, if it can be helped. Whatever happens, don't let anyone open that note. You understand?'

Charley understood, but he was apprehensive about the ranch being weakened by his absence. 'Suppose them soldiers is already on their way? Suppose John gets up a big, fighting posse, and come—?'

'Just go,' exclaimed George, a little irritably. 'Don't get caught, deliver the note, then get back here.'

Charley headed for the barn, worried and a little baffled. He did not turn to see Jeff and Young Jim join George on the front veranda, but when he emerged from the barn leading his saddled horse, he looked sardonically out where the spy to the east was squatting in sunlight beside his drowsing horse. As he loped from the yard that watcher arose and stared, seemingly torn between a desire to follow and see what Charley Wagner was up to, or stay and make certain the remaining Circle H men did not use Charley as a ruse so they could spirit the Indian girl away.

In the end, the horseman stayed, and as Charley raced for town below him, he derisively waved a hand.

Jeff and George returned to the corral where those big green horses were, attempting to at least go through the motions of working.

Young Jim returned to Elena's room. She looked like she might have been crying, but he did not ask and she volunteered nothing. He smiled from the doorway. 'When you're able to ride, maybe I can get a couple of horses from George, and maybe a pack outfit, and we could go exploring around in the mountains for a couple of weeks.'

She stared at him.

'Well,' he said, 'you don't want to go back, do you?'

'No.'

'Well, then you'll be free, when you're able to get around again, and me, I got some days off coming. We could fish the high-country lakes, and explore the forests, and find a mountaintop to sit on in the sunshine, and just do nothing if we didn't want to.'

She laughed at him. They were the same age, but in

the kind of things she was thinking now, she was older; she was instinctively more knowledgeable. But she still smiled.

'All right, Young Jim, if you want to I'll go with you.'

They talked away an hour and a half, and when he left, this time, in response to Amos's bawling tones outside, she held his hand again. This time, she squeezed his fingers. This time, he squeezed back.

Amos was on the cookshack porch like a stork standing in hot water. He fidgeted, jumped up and down, and waved his arms as he kept bellowing for George and Jeff. The moment Young Jim stepped out beside him, Amos grabbed the lanky youth, dragged him around, and made him look out where Amos was rigidly pointing.

'Soldiers! Two gawd-damned ranks of 'em,' bawled Amos, and turned as George and Jeff came up. 'Look yonder. They even got their blasted cannon, or whatever it is, with 'em . . . By golly, George, we got to get hold of that cannon. If we don't, and they set back out there and shell us . . .' Amos rolled up his eyes, then dropped them. 'My buffler rifle'll reach that far, neat as a whistle. I'll fetch it.'

'Wait a minute,' Hinman said, grabbing Amos's arm as the *cosinero* started past. 'Settle down.' George let go of Amos's arm and leaned on the porch railing, studying the slowly advancing, orderly column. 'How in hell did they get up here so fast?' He mused aloud. 'I didn't expect them until a lot later, or maybe in the morning.'

Amos, restrained from going after his rifle, remained agitated. 'Never mind the speculations. We got to get set

134

for defense. Boys, we got to lay out all the weapons and shell-boxes. We got to barricade the house.'

Jeff and George turned slow stares in Amos's direction. Even Young Jim was intrigued by the older man's agitation. Through the sudden silence on the porch a man's high call floated down through the afternoon. Immediately Amos squinted. 'He's orderin' up the cannon, boys. He's goin' to set out there and bombard the hell out of us!'

The column kept on moving. It only halted once, when those two spies left their positions to report to Captain Potter. Jeff sighed. 'Now he'll know Charley's gone, and that whittles down the odds.'

'Not by much,' said George, dryly. 'Sixty troopers and a howitzer against four men, or five, don't make much difference.' He turned on Amos. 'Don't you do anything that's going to start this war,' he warned. 'Don't bring out that damned buffler gun, either. Get one of the shotguns, and take the lad with you so's he can get a Winchester, then the pair of you stay right here in the cookshack. The only time you use a gun is if some soldier tries to come inside.'

George turned towards his rangeboss. 'You mind the front veranda, and the front door. No one comes in.'

Jeff understood. 'Where'll you be?' he asked, and George pointed. 'Out in the yard, yonder.'

'That's plumb exposed,' protested Jeff.

George smiled at them. 'Damned if it isn't. But we're not going to fight them—there's no way we could win like that, we're goin' to out-fox them.'

He strolled out of the cookshack without explaining.

They watched him go without a word, then Amos and Young Jim trooped back to the parlor wall-rack to re-arm themselves, and Jeff took up his position near the front doorway. He could see out into the yard from there, and what he saw was George cross down as far as the tie-rack in front of the big log barn, turn, and settle against the rack as the company of cavalrymen was halted just beyond the yard, while Captain Potter came on alone, and now the officer had both a holstered pistol on his broad, shiny belt, and a long cavalry saber.

George nodded when Potter halted, and amiably said, 'Your men made good time from Rabbit-Ear Pass, Captain.'

Potter sighed. 'What's the sense of all this, Mister Hinman, I don't want to fight you.'

George smiled. 'That's good, because we sure don't want to fight you either.'

Potter gestured towards the distant mountains. 'We're supposed to go up in there tomorrow and chouse out some reservation-jumpers. We're supposed to herd them back up north.' He clasped both hands atop the saddlehorn and stolidly gazed at George. 'I don't want trouble with them, or with you. I just want to do my duty, and head on back. The Indian girl is part of that band of break-outs. She's got to go back just like the others. Mister Hinman, just give her up and take my word for it, she'll be treated as well as anyone else.'

'Captain, she don't want to go back to the reservation. She told me that. I figure, where we're miles apart, is that I see her as a woman, as a person, and you see her as a break-out.'

136

Captain Potter rolled his eyes. 'We're back to that again. Mister Hinman, there's no point arguing about this. I've got my orders. They *all* go back. Every one of them is a ward of the government. That's all there is to it.'

The sun was dropping, there were shadows now. Time had passed of which none of the men on Circle H had been aware. Almost the entire day was gone. Charley had left hours earlier. They had first spied the troops an hour earlier. A lot of time had passed, but it did not seem that it had. In crises, time somehow always got compressed until hours seemed no longer than moments.

George finally said something that indicated he might be facing up to a change of heart. 'Captain, I need an hour or so to think about this.'

Potter's expression changed instantly, it showed hope. 'Take all the time you need, Mister Hinman. Mind if we water our horses at your trough?'

George did not mind at all. He strolled slowly back in the direction of the house, while Captain Potter rode almost as slowly back in the direction of his horse-holding cavalrymen.

When George walked into the parlor, he said, 'Jeff; go out there and keep watch for Charley. The minute you see him, let me know.'

Jeff departed, trailing a carbine, and George strolled on through to visit Elena. He was in there with her for almost the entire hour. He did not emerge, in fact, until Jeff came rushing inside to yell that he had seen Charley coming back, in a run.

George finally went to the cookshack where Amos

was nervously drinking one cup of coffee after another, and where Young Jim was leaning in the doorway, watching the soldiers.

George and Young Jim saw Charley coming. There was a second horseman riding all over his racing mount, like a big, flopping scarecrow, farther back. No one knew who he was, but George, and all he said, as he stepped back inside, was: 'Young Jim, help them stall the horses, then bring 'em both straight on up to the house.'

Charley cut wide out and around the interested soldiers, who watched with frank curiosity as he raced on around them towards the yard, the scarecrow behind him, following Charley's same route into the yard.

Chapter Seventeen
GEORGE HINMAN'S VICTORY

The soldiers rode in, loosely, and dismounted to water their animals. Young Jim was surprised because many of them looked no older than he was. He smiled, tentatively, and they smiled back.

Then Charley and the scarecrow who had been following him, came up, riding a stiff-legged, wary trot, and Young Jim headed for the barn to help with the horses. Charley was tense as a coiled spring, but the lanky, older man who rode right on down into the barn before dismounting, seemed more relieved at abandoning his saddle than upset over finding the ranch-yard full of armed cavalrymen.

Charley said, 'What's happened?' and Young Jim

answered curtly. 'Nothing. Yet. George said for you two fellers to get right on over to the house.'

Charley, like most stockmen, functioned largely by instinct. He cared for his horse, first, then he walked out of the barn with the lanky older man and Young Jim, heading for the main-house. He did not look anything but apprehensive as they walked among the unconcerned cavalrymen. When they reached the house Charley paused at the door to look back. He shook his head, then trooped on inside.

George and Jeff were waiting. The lanky, rumpled older man offered George his hand. 'It's been quite a spell,' he said. 'Six, seven years, George, since I been in this house.'

George nodded, shook, then turned towards Young Jim and Charley Wagner. 'That officer out there is going to be coming along directly. He allowed me an hour and I've already run over it by some.' George paused, put his full attention upon Young Jim, and said, 'Son; this here is your wedding day.'

Everyone except the lanky older man looked stunned.

'I said they aren't going to take her, and they aren't,' stated George, looking steadily at Young Jim. 'Seven years ago I had the same trouble. That's when I married my wife, and I never knew a finer woman.'

Jeff weakly said, 'Wait a minute . . . Young Jim and *her?*'

George nodded. 'This here is the parson from Kremmling. He'll marry 'em. Elena is ready. We talked about it for an hour. She's plumb ready and willing.' George looked straight at Young Jim again. 'Son; you can cut loose later, if you want to. She understands that, and you should also understand it. The way this works is pretty simple. I know, I found it out seven years back. The minute Elena marries you, Young Jim, she ceases being a ward of the government. She becomes your wife—a citizen of the country. Those soldiers out there can no more move her against her will than they can move any of the rest of us, unless we've broke a federal law, and there's no law against a Crow woman marrying a white man. I know!'

Charley recovered first. He looked at Young Jim with a crooked little grin. 'Congratulations, son. You know— you're a lucky buck. That's about the prettiest woman—red *or* white—I ever saw.'

Young Jim turned red, then he gradually got pale. When he could finally speak, he said, 'George; she don't love me, and I . . .'

'Yes? What about you?'

'. . . I don't know, what about me,' muttered the youth.

'She's not pretty as a picture, son?'

'Yes sir, she's that pretty, and then some.'

'Then what is it?'

'I never much thought about owning a wife. I can't keep one, on what I make.'

'Sure you can,' exclaimed George. 'You're a tophand now. Just since this afternoon, with tophand wages.' George lay a hand upon Young Jim's shoulder and gave him a gentle shove. 'Go on with the parson, son. Jeff, you and Charley go along as witnesses and the Best Man.' He dropped his hand and smiled at the lanky youth. 'Take my word for it, that girl in there will teach you how to laugh all over again . . . And other things.'

The minister reached for Young Jim's arm, Jeff and Charley stepped in behind him, in case he needed a little steadying on the way to the bedroom, and George picked up his hat, dumped it upon the back of his head, and walked resolutely out to the front veranda, then on down to the yard in the direction of Captain Potter, who was standing beside a large black horse, talking to a grizzled, red-headed Irish sergeant.

Potter turned away from the sergeant the moment he saw George approaching, his expression showing a mixture of feelings, but predominantly hope. He even smiled at George as he said, 'Well, Mister Hinman?'

George smiled back. 'You can ride out any time you're of a mind to, Captain. We don't have anything to decide, not any more.'

Potter's brows pulled downward a notch. 'Don't we? Where is the girl?'

'She is marrying one of my riders, Captain.'

Evidently Captain Potter did not require an explanation, because he stood gazing steadily at George for a long moment, then he said, 'That *was* a preacher, then. The sergeant was just telling me who the second man was who just rode in.'

George and the red-headed sergeant exchanged a look. The sergeant's eyes showed keen amusement, but he did not say a word. 'I'll send out the preacher,' said George, 'so you can verify that the marriage was performed legal-like and all.'

Captain Potter shrugged thick shoulders. 'All right, Mister Hinman. You know, I'm glad in a way. I didn't want to be burdened by an injured Indian, but mainly, I feel a little like you do—they're entitled to more freedom of choice than they're getting.' He offered his hand and George shook it, then turned back towards the house as Captain Potter turned again to his sergeant.

'We can make it back to Kremmling before dark, if we hurry, Sergeant. Then in the morning we can head into the mountains. Get the men to horse.'

Amos met George at the front door and for once his voice was neither strident nor bitter. 'I never did that before,' he said softly. 'I never kissed a bride before— and her sort of weeping and all.'

George nodded. 'Amos, you heard of shotgun weddings?'

'Yes, of course.'

'Well, you just stood up at a *howitzer* wedding. I don't figure very many folks ever do *that!*'

The preacher came into the parlor pocketing his Good Book and beaming. Behind him came Charley and Jeff, both of whom looked uniquely soft around the eyes and lips. George handed the minister a greenback and sent Amos with him to the barn to see the minister on his way. He then turned to Charley. 'You kissed the bride too?'

Charley nodded without commenting on this—it was too embarrassing, but when George started past, Charley grabbed his arm. 'Leave 'em be, George. She's snifflin' and he's standing there like a pole-axed steer. But when we was leaving he started talking about some trip to the high-country for a couple of weeks, with a pack outfit, as soon as she's fit to ride.'

George turned back. 'Where did Amos put that bottle of popskull he keeps in the cookshack?'

Neither of the other rangemen answered, but they trooped along in the wake of their employer to help ransack the cupboards until they found it.

Center Point Publishing
600 Brooks Road • PO Box 1
Thorndike ME 04986-0001 USA

(207) 568-3717

US & Canada:
1 800 929-9108